Praise for Malaika Favorite

"Though speculative in nature, *The Author Project* presents familiar behaviors and tendencies that give uncanny glimpses and reflections of current events readers will easily recognize."
—Gina Ferrara, author of *Weight of the Ripened*, editor for *New Orleans Poetry Review*

"Provocative and deeply engrossing. This fast-paced book will make readers question today's decisions and their impact on the future."
—Frank Stewart, author of *Time Will Tell: Studies in African American History*

"The thesis of this novella is incredibly powerful and the writing inviting."
—Philip Kolin, distinguished Professor Emeritus and author of over 40 books on Shakespeare and Tennessee Williams

"Some stories are full of truth. Some of magic, or beauty, or knowledge, or foresight. Malaika Favorite's new novella, *The Author Project,* is full of all of these, at once, on every page. This book lays bare so much about human nature, ambition, greed, technology, politics, survival, and life, there's nothing to do but read it wide-eyed and nodding in agreement first page to last. Favorite's gifts have always been her vision, her imagery, and her ability to craft immaculate language into clear, honest narrative. *The Author Project* contains these gifts in abundance, and for all of them, for this author, I am very grateful."
—Jack B. Bedell, author of *Ghost Forest*, Poet Laureate of Louisiana, 2017-2019

The Author Project

Malaika Favorite

**Winner of the
Moon Meridian Novella Award**

-First Edition

Publisher's Cataloguing-in-Publication Data

Favorite, Malaika
    The author project / written by Malaika Favorite
    ISBN: 978-1-953932-24-2

1. Fiction: General 2. Fiction: Science Fiction - General 3. Fiction: Science Fiction - Humorous I. Title II. Author

Library of Congress Control Number: 2023951635

Dedicated to my husband,
Anthony Kellman,
who believed in my magic.

Chapter One

Once or twice a month I visit my hiding place. A secluded spot up in the mountains away from the world of political intrigue. When I was looking for a place, I told the agent I wanted a hunting lodge; something simple, no electricity, just a fireplace for heat and water to drink. She found one with three simple rooms, a fireplace, a wood stove for cooking, and an old hand water pump. Very few people come up here and only if I invite them. I can't describe the peace I feel when I'm here. If I ever decide to kill myself, I will do it right outside this cabin, and die slowly, watching the stars.

My mother named me Luke Adam Voss because she expected me to grow up and be like Dr. Luke in the bible. And because I was her first son she threw in Adam. As a small boy, my mother bought medical books and gave them to me to play with. The books had pictures of medical equipment and different kinds of medicines. When I could read, she insisted I study the history of black doctors and quizzed me on what I read. She was determined to get a doctor out of me, but unfortunately, I failed her and got an MBA focusing on technology and business management. To this day I regret that choice. I often say to myself that I'm glad she died right after I graduated with my MBA degree. I would not want her to know the man I became. It is possible she would applaud me, like so many other women do, but there is no Luke in me for her to admire.

I have an old manual typewriter up here; I use it to peck away at my memoir that I plan to deliver to the world, eventually. Writing all this down helps me to understand how it happened, how the situation blindsided me and altered my life forever. Most people who meet me envy my life and my potential; however, I am embarrassed to admit how I got to the top of this mountain. I was naïve; I did not foresee the outcome of my actions.

I was an assistant to a great man, Author C. Owen. He entrusted me with his legacy, his creation. He asked me on that last day to take care of Author as if Author, the machine, were a child he was leaving behind in our care. He asked me to see to it that the Author Project was fully realized. At the time, I believed in the Author Project. When he was alive, Author touted it as the ultimate solution to world peace. I did not think it could achieve world peace, but I did believe it could conceivably improve how we did things and how we interacted with machines. I believed that artificial intelligence held an untapped potential that could revolutionize the modern world. I was thinking about ending hunger at home and in underdeveloped countries. I was hoping I could approach my mother's grave and say: Mom, I am now in the annals of great black doctors who saved humanity. And I did it without getting a medical degree. I have earned my name.

I could blame Author for dying on us. In fact, I did blame him for a long time, but now I blame him for different reasons. I was attempting to do my job with the help of my coworkers. Conversely, it all backfired on us, and now our lives are complicated. This small sliver of peace is all I get; whenever I can, I sneak off and hide up here. I accept the blame for credulously allowing things to get out of hand, though I often wonder if I ever had anything in hand. More and more I believe it was never in my hegemony in the first place. I am convinced I was a pawn under the influence of a diabolical force.

I was the first to propose the idea to enter Author in the race for the presidency. It was a joke made while listening to the debates. We were at a get-together at Tenisha's place eating pizza and watching the debates between the Democrats, Republicans, and one Independent candidate. We were employed at the Special Projects Office, a sort of think-tank established by the government to do research on the advanced utilization of computer-generated technology, i.e., artificial intelligence. Our former boss, Author C. Owen, now deceased, developed the project and left us in charge to continue his research. Originally, there were twelve of us. He called us his disciples and we felt proud to be his followers, though we were not sure what would happen to his research now that he was gone.

There were only six of us at the party: Tenisha Powers, Kim Lee Su, Patricia Spooner, Amos Baxter, Javier Fernandez, and me, Luke Voss. I did not feel much like a part of the team, as I did not consider myself a genius in any field. I knew something about technology, but my specialty was business and organization, a trait often lacking in the genius class. Javier Fernandez was a specialist in plasma physics and nuclear fusion as it relates to technology. Javier was married with four kids or was it six? I lost count after his wife said she thought she was pregnant with twins or multiples and they had not had the ultrasound yet. Kim Lee was also a family man with two kids; his special focus was Engineering Physics. Pat and Amos were both computer scientists who specialize in Human–computer interactions and genetic engineering. They were stuck somewhere between living together and maybe marrying soon. When I discussed the matter with Pat, she said it was marrying soon, but when I talked to Amos, he said marriage was a serious commitment that required a larger brain permutation than the two of them could fit into a minivan. That made no sense to me, but I think it had something to do with who was the brainier of the two, an issue they could not agree on. That leaves Tenisha, her specialty being genetics, nanotechnology, and robotics with a focus on interactive design as it relates to human and computer interfaces with direct implant technology. What can I say about Tenisha Powers? She has always been an enigma to me. She was very smart and sexy when she wanted to be; anyway, we were in an off-and-on relationship, depending on Tenisha's mood. She was my type of woman, but maybe my brain did not fit in her Lexus mind.

We were the closest members of Author's team, the others technical support people; we called them the super-tech-squadron because all they did was connect wires and assemble and disassemble computer components and such. Their job was just as important as ours, but they were not the brains behind the project; they just did the labor. I was the person who passed out notebooks, took notes, kept records, and organized information into a database. I was not as dedicated to Author as the others were. I believed in the project, but personally, I felt it was time to move on to new endeavors and forget the Author Project. Conversely, there was the matter of what to do about the plan. We argued over what Author the First meant about fully realizing the Author Project. I felt he wanted us to continue research on the Author Project and explore how to use it in advanced technology and robotics.

When he told us he had prostate cancer and did not have much time left, the others argued that he was hoping to be installed in the Author program as a part of the Author computer and that he expected us to bring him back from the dead as the living mind of Author. I told them their ideas were from science fiction, and I did not think we needed another Frankenstein monster in the world, even if it was a machine.

Aside from our disagreements about how to proceed with the Author Project, we got along pretty well for a diverse group of people working on the same undefined mission. We considered continuing without the Author Project as our focus, but we did not want the government to shut us down for lack of leadership and direction. After all, who or what company would hire us given the nature of our resumes? In addition, the government grant Author left us was substantial, and I was in charge of filing the progress reports, usually based on a combination of vague promises that Author thought up while having a martini break. My next report was due at the end of the quarter, and I had nothing to report other than our disagreements about what to do next. My proposal was to put Author, the computer, in mothballs until we had proof that it was an operational model, and until we understood exactly what Author wanted us to do with it. This brought on another level of disagreements because it seems, Author the First left conflicting instructions with each member of the team.

He told Tenisha he wanted the Author creation to be a sort of overseer of government projects that could fact-check proposals and study the sustainability and usefulness of each application. This was the information I elaborated on in my last quarterly report. The contradiction was evident when Pat told us that he had her and Amos working on a data processing system that would allow the Author program to interact with any computer. He expected them to design a program that would allow entrance into the human mind by combining it with a sort of touch-and-receive system, whereby you touch a surface and the computer reads your mind and delivers what you want. Amos said the technique was scary because it could work in reverse, whereby you read the computer's mind and obey what it wants you to do or think. He felt it was a sort of mind-control device that did not work too well.

Author told Javier and Kim Su that he was interested in the Author creation being used to generate electromagnetic fields from the environment that could be used like electrical charges to jumpstart the mind to do amazing things. Javier went into the complicated process of thermonuclear fusion with matter and the mind as a ball of kinetic energy that could be altered to achieve a sort of super mind. He and Kim Su were working on this project to assist Author in creating the super-mind when the transfer happened.

Author the First was the subject, and they were conducting an experiment that would allow an electromagnetic force to enter Author's brain and stimulate it to increase productivity. Javier told us that Author kept insisting that they pump in more juice, as they called it, and eventually his body short-circuited and he died. Javier blamed himself for Author's death. He wanted to turn himself in for involuntary manslaughter. We had a difficult time convincing him that Author caused his own death.

Kim insisted that Author did it on purpose, that he wanted to die at that moment so his brain would somehow transfer into the computer program. I am not sure how true that is, but I do know that he told me right before his death I would soon be in touch with the most powerful computer in the world, and that was when he asked me to take care of Author and see to it that the Author Project was fully realized. When I look back on the conversation, I believe I said something like, "If I was in touch with the most powerful computer in the world, I don't think it would need a mere mortal like me." He had laughed and winked at me as if he knew something I did not know, and that's why I agreed with Kim Su that he committed intellectual suicide. The fool fried his own brain, or shall I say he overcooked it in a microwave machine that rendered it useless for all practical purposes?

When it happened, Kim yelled for us to get the Defibrillator. We tried our best to revive Author, but it was obvious he was gone. His head was literally smoking, or the wires attached to his head were smoking and some had melted. Javier broke down crying, yelling that they had murdered him and it was their fault. He told Kim to stop; he said he yelled for Kim to stop pumping the electromagnetic fields into the machine, but Kim said Author begged for more, he kept saying, just a little more boys, just a little more. Later Kim confessed that Author had pulled him aside before the procedure and told him to keep pumping no matter the outcome. He made Kim promise that he would not stop pumping as long as there was electromagnetic power flowing from the machine. I felt sorry for Javier. It took him a long while to accept that he was not guilty of murder. He even confessed to his priest who absolved him of all guilt, and that helped in his recovery. Kim, on the other hand, wanted to quit the project. He and his wife had already packed when he gave me his resignation. We all surrounded him and informed him that he could not leave us alone with an incomplete project. He reluctantly agreed to remain until we got the project back in functional mode.

Chapter Two

IT WAS EARLY IN THE PRESIDENTIAL RACE when we met at Tenisha's home. We wanted to decide which candidate we would back with our money and our endorsements since we wanted someone in office who sounded like they were partial to technology and would be in favor of keeping our project in the money. This had nothing to do with our pending report; it was just an excuse to look here and there for sources of funding if we lost our government contract. We were feeling desperate and fearful for our future. It was important to support the right candidate with our money and visible presence just in case we needed them to insure the future of the Author Project. We knew we were running out of time, and the less time we had, the more often we felt we had to meet after office hours.

Kim Lee suggested we close down the office, take a long-awaited vacation, then make a decision after our minds were refreshed and inspired by idle thinking. Tenisha suggested we have a get-together to review the candidates for the upcoming election since we would eventually have to convince him or her of our usefulness in government service. So, there we were, lounging around at Tenisha's house, joking, drinking, eating, and void of any useful ideas for our future. Once more, we had postponed a decision. I suggested I jiggle some words around and repeat what Author had promised in an earlier report. The others agreed, if necessary, that was what we would do. We sat on the sofa and some on the floor and watched the presidential debate, knowing in the back of our minds we had not come close to resolving our desperate situation. We were reminiscing a great deal of late, just to keep our minds off what had happened to our boss and how to proceed without him.

"Both parties are weak if you ask me," Javier said.

I was already tipsy and I needed a laugh since Tenisha was ignoring my advances. Tenisha had on a short skirt and I was having trouble resisting her. Every time I accidentally rested my hand on her smooth thigh, she kicked me, and I was rather enjoying the game. I was half listening to the woman on the screen who was making a list of promises that were as old as the presidential promises dished out ten years ago. "We should enter Author into the race," I said humorously to a good laugh. There was a moment of pregnant silence as if we were pledging a unified agreement in our minds. It was a beautiful moment, a kind of integrated enlightenment, as the idea of a temporary solution to our quandary occurred to each of us at the same time. I said, "We could at least try it for fun."

Amos laughed and got up to go to the restroom. He had been drinking a lot since Author died. He told me he did not want to look for another job and I should find a solution soon or he might develop a liver disease from alcoholism. Pat reached over and squeezed my leg; she was sitting on the floor, leaning on the edge of the sofa. Her red hair hung down her back almost touching the floor. She and Amos looked as if they were related; we often teased them and called them the Scottish twins.

She looked up at me. "Maybe it's a good idea, Luke. I mean, they want us to develop advanced technological use for supercomputers. Proposing the Author Project as a test of our supercomputer could keep them off our backs for a while, and in the meantime, we could debate possible solutions of what we should really do with the project." She stared into space smiling. "I can see the headlines now, A COMPUTER AS PRESIDENT, IS IT TIME OR IS IT TIME WASTED?" Then she burst out laughing. "Luke, you're more of a genius than you realize.'

When Amos returned from the restroom, we had a candidate to enter the presidential race. Pat repeated the proposal to Amos. Javier said it would buy us some time and Kim agreed. Tenisha was hesitant; she felt it was disrespectful to Author to make a jest of his lifelong work. I reassured her that it was just for fun and that Author would appreciate a good joke.

Amos reminded us that Author was officially dead and he felt the plan was ludicrous. We argued over the issue for two or three hours, debated the pros and cons, wrote them down on yellow pads, and then we voted. Tenisha was averse to exposing the Author Project to public scrutiny, but I reminded her that keeping her job was more important than public scrutiny. She was the only one holding out, but when I mentioned her job, she quickly changed her vote.

Once we made the initial decision, we set up a grid on the computer to track Author's progress as a viable candidate. That was the extent of our plan; we did not expect any results, except a good laugh and time to devise our approach on how to use the Author Project, if at all. In addition, we were hoping to get some media coverage to stress the importance of our project and its usefulness in governmental affairs. Author would be a write-in candidate and I would act as his campaign manager, to amuse myself.

Let me make it clear; none of us expected Author to win anything other than a few sly remarks on late-night shows. It was a hoax; we placed bets on how many votes Author would get as a write-in candidate, so to speak. We waged a dollar for each vote we thought he would get with the money going to the one who got the closest guess.

Chapter Three

ASTONISHINGLY, SOMETHING HAPPENED, something out of the ordinary, and to this day, I cannot explain it. I think it happened after I introduced Author or the concept of Author as a candidate in the race for president. I made the proposal in a New York Times article, thinking people would get the prank and we would get some free publicity from the media. I made an elaborate case for the Author Project and AI as a new direction for the future of politics in America. I proposed it as a solution to world problems and domestic issues. I must say, it had a ring of possibility, but in the back of my mind, I knew I was playing a game and soon the press would expose the absurdity of the idea. Nevertheless, by then we would have bought some time and interest in funding for the Project as a solution for resolving domestic and international difficulties. Unexpectedly, it did not happen as I planned.

CNN invited me to do a half-hour interview about the Author Project. I explained the project in non-technical language as if I knew what I was talking about; in truth, I was inventing as I talked. I imagined that the Author team was watching me on TV and praying I would shut up before I said something totally absurd. The moderator, Larry Duvall, thought I was serious, and people all over America were interested in knowing more about Author. The switchboards were jammed with callers and Author became an overnight celebrity. Then things got out of my control. It was as if Author took over his own campaign and I was just there to introduce him. Still, I was not convinced he would win anything except a few laughs.

My job description changed. I was now the official spokesperson for the group and assigned the task of extending the game. The more we played the Author card, the more attention we earned for the project. When Larry Duvall asked for a second interview, I wanted to call it quits, but the others thought we should see how far the game would go. They encouraged me to accept with the intention of begging for additional funding. I started my introductory remarks by emphasizing the importance of computer technology in an advanced society and boldly stated that we were ahead of other countries in computer and genetic technology. I stressed that it was necessary to take an audacious step to advance the cause of genetic engineering. I tried to avoid the issue of a machine as our national leader since in my heart I felt it was an incongruous idea. Larry wanted to bring the focus back to the presidential race since that was the hot topic being debated by the pundits.

"Do you really believe the American people will vote for an AI machine over a man or woman for President, Mr. Voss? Aren't you being a bit ridiculous?" That was his reply to my long-winded discussion about genetics and computer technology. I took it as an affront to my intelligence. I was determined to verbally insult him and extended my argument for an AI machine as a leader.

"You must understand, Larry, Author is not just any machine. It is the most powerful computer in the whole world. We programmed Author with all the knowledge of humankind. Author's database is from historical documents and libraries throughout the world. Unlike most humans, Author has read and retained every book in every language on every subject. Author can check his databank for comparative information so that he will always make the best possible decision. Remember the old cliché, 'history teaches that man does not learn from history;' you see, man may not learn from history but computers do." I smiled, congratulating myself on my wit and the fact that I had read all the reports on what was downloaded into the Author Project.

"But Author has no feelings," Larry argued.

"Precisely, that is the point; his lack of emotions makes him an ideal leader. Think about it, Larry, with Author as president, we would save a ton of money, the economy would grow to boundless proportions, the government would be less expensive."

"What exactly do you mean by that?"

"Well, Author will work for free; his salary will go toward extinguishing the national debt. He requires no food or sleeping quarters. The White House will become a temporary museum. As long as Author is president, no one will live there. There will be no need for the Secret Service because Author will monitor his own security. There will be no White House scandals, I mean, you know, the usual stuff that can happen between men and women in a place of power." I laughed, and since I felt I was on slippery ice, I changed the subject. "Author is also equipped with a self-check device that is programmed to keep track of any glitches in the system."

Larry smirked as if he had one of those I-got-you questions, "Suppose, for argument's sake, that Author is hacked, then the United States will be controlled by a terroristic regime?"

I smiled and reared back in my chair, "That will never happen because Author is the original hacker. No one or nothing can hack a machine that hacks first, if you know what I mean."

"No, I don't know what you mean, please elaborate."

I leaned forward, "Right now, as we discuss Author's abilities, I invite every hacker and computer wizard in the world to make an attempt to hack into Author's system and change one page of data. I invite them to send results by the end of this program. If any person or any machine is able to get into the Author computer, then I myself will concede on behalf of Author and give up the race." That was a bold move, but I was high on power at the time; it's a wonder I didn't make even greater promises. In my mind, I could see Amos cursing me out and Pat trying to calm him down while Kim Su was probably yelling to his wife that Voss has made a complete fool of himself on national TV.

"That's a bold challenge, Mr. Voss." He then stared directly at the camera. "To all you hackers and computer geniuses, the clock is ticking. Let's see if anyone can get into the Author program. In the meantime, I have another question for you, Mr. Voss. Since you are the speaker for Author, will every question and answer during a debate have to go through you?"

I was somewhat taken aback by that one, but I boldly answered, "No, Author will and can speak for himself." I wasn't sure if that was exactly true or possible, but I figured we could program him to answer all questions asked, and if necessary, we, as a team, could respond for the machine.

Larry wasn't through with me; he was determined to cancel Author as a viable contender. "If we close down the White House, what will happen to the staff and all the people who are now employed to protect the president and his family? I would think your plan would increase the unemployment numbers."

I felt weak for a moment, but I quickly regained my sense of purpose and thought up a convenient lie. "Not really, Author will study their profiles and place them in jobs suited to their experience with salaries commensurate with their former pay. Of course, we will need to maintain a skeletal crew on staff for basic upkeep and to manage the visitors coming to view a historic building." I knew this was a weak argument and I had to wiggle my way out of explaining how this displacement-replacement policy would benefit the country. "I foresee men and women who now serve in mundane jobs being retrained to use their minds to the fullest possible extent. After all, for the past fifty or so years, we have continued to use the same outdated systems while computer-generated technology has surpassed us in our slow path to upward mobility. With the Author Project, we hope to retrain government officials and set a new and efficient order of governmental services in motion." Larry stared at me as if he was thinking, *Yeah, I've heard that lie before,* but his next question threw me off guard. I had to think fast for an answer, and I was praying for a commercial break.

He asked, "Mr. Voss, can we trust a machine with our national secrets?"

I wrote a note on the pad in front of me asking for a commercial break; however, before I was able to slip the note to Larry, I had a rebuttal to the question. I folded the piece of paper up as if I was scribbling a reminder to my staff. I slowly placed it in my pocket, folded my hands on the table, and leaned forward. "We can trust a machine; we've been trusting people for thousands of years, and look at the mess that has gotten us into. Furthermore, in an effort to improve our human deficiencies, we have relied on machines every day with every secret we have. By electing Author, we will be giving the machine a name and a title as opposed to pretending that men and women are storing, sorting, and evaluating our sensitive information."

Larry smiled as if he was planning to ask for my phone number or my bank account number; instead, he asked, "Where does Author live?"

"That, my friend, is top secret information. For the interest of the country, we find it necessary to keep Author's base of operation confidential, and only a few people know where that is." I fixed my face as if to say, that's all you're getting out of me on that subject. The truth was more frightening than I wanted to admit, even to myself. The original Author told me that he designed Author on the principle of a computer virus; therefore, he is everywhere at once, or shall we say, omnipresent. If the world knew about that, it would give more fuel to those who believed that the Author computer is the anti-Christ set in motion by a committee of secret leaders attempting to take over the whole world. The other top-secret information I knew was that Author was the most powerful computer networking system in the known world. According to the original Author, it was impossible to destroy the Author program and impossible to hide from him. Everyone who had any type of computer device or cell phone or any item communicating by satellite was also connected to Author, and yes, Author was watching, and this scared the hell out of me.

"When will we meet this Author C. Owens? Will he be available for debates and interviews?"

"Yes, of course, we are in the process of outfitting Author with the necessary equipment to perform that task," I lied. I imagined that Author was outfitting himself as we were speaking. Pat informed me that there was some unusual activity going on with the Author program. She and Amos noted that many of the older files had been altered and updated on a regular basis.

"Mr. Voss, don't you think it would be better if Author at least looked like a man or a woman?"

"We considered that idea, but Author objected. He feels it is time for Americans to accept advanced technology via AI as a part of our social and political environment."

"What exactly do you mean by accepting advanced technology? We already depend on our cell phones and computers; isn't that advanced enough?"

"I think Author wants us to accept machines as natural leaders, not to pretend that the machine is some dressed-up contraption from a sci-fi movie."

"Then what's the point of calling him Author? Why not Mindy #2, or Sue #506, or just machine #402, or something like that?"

"We examined that possibility, but we felt it would help our cause by allowing Author to use his given name of Author C. Owen. He was named after his creator, Author Owen, who donated his living brain for the creation of the project. The process of absorption was so powerful it caused a complete demolition of the original Author's body and mind. Author absorbed everything that his creator knew and can maintain digital functions completely without help from any of us. Thus, Author the man, in a sense, became Author the machine, not far removed from humans, just more invincible," I smiled as I trembled at the thought of what I had just said.

"Does Author have a degree from an established university?"

"Author has studied every course available and completed curriculums from every accredited university in the world, and he has retained all he has learned. Literally speaking, he has a PhD in every conceivable field of knowledge."

"So, how do we know your Author won't turn on us, and like machines in the movies independently decide to destroy all humans?"

I laughed and shifted in my seat. "Larry, don't be dramatic. Author is programmed to act in the best interest of humankind in general and America in particular. Author is a total patriot, an authentic American, a true Made in America believer in all we stand for and fought and died for."

During the break, Larry whispered to me with his mike off, "Are you sure you want to continue with this?" That was my chance to opt out of the whole fiasco, but I was high on my aptitude for persuasion and I said yes, let's do it.

Larry faced the camera. "This is astounding. Who would have thought that this would be possible in our lifetime? Ladies and gentlemen: we will now greet Author C. Owen, and according to my understanding,

Author does not show up for interviews but is stationary, locked away in a hidden location, and will appear to us via satellite. Is that right?"

"That's correct. We will continue the discussion via a special satellite computer imaging program," I confirmed.

"Author, are you with us?" Larry asked.

"Yes, I am. Greetings to you, Mr. Duvall, and greetings to the American people."

"What am I seeing on the screen, Mr. Voss?"

"What you are seeing is Author himself, his brain in action, all those colors are neurons firing thoughts our way; in essence, you are seeing the mind of Author C. Owen."

"Author, I will allow you to introduce yourself as you see fit and explain to the American people who or what you are and how you can work for them," Larry said.

Author the AI machine took over as if he had been waiting for this opportunity, and at that moment, Author the AI boldly declared its ability to speak freely without help from me and I became his second in command.

"Before I proceed to explain myself, let me first shut down the hackers attempting to enter my data system. To prove that I am on the ball and have the power to do this, I will expose them as I shut them down. I will also do a printout of their names, addresses, and computer login information for our governmental authorities to investigate and deal with as they see fit. Please excuse me for a brief interval of necessary computer counterintelligence." He paused as if he had read Larry's mind. "Please do not do a commercial break; these people need to be exposed publically."

I was shocked; I did not expect that reply from Author the program. I knew the team had wired him to greet the TV audience and to say something profound and intelligent, but I did not expect this. I presumed the hackers would try to get into the program and fail, then we would announce that no one was able to hack into the Author program. I sucked my teeth and pretended I was in agreement with Author's actions. There was a brief flashing of lights, then one by one, the hackers were exposed, their startled faces staring at their computer screens as they saw themselves unveiled on national TV. Many quickly covered their faces or ran from the rooms they were in as their basic information was printed out on the screen. Larry and I both sat watching in a state of startled amazement. Finally, after frantic signals from the TV station producer, Larry closed the show.

"Ladies and gentlemen, this ends our program for the night. We look forward to further conversations with—with the AI computer, Author C. Owen."

Chapter Four

AFTER A FEW INTERVIEWS, I noticed what Author the computer was doing. He gave his speeches supplemented with visual impressions that happened so fast you were not sure if you thought them up or saw them on the screen. His approval ratings were at an all-time high, 85% and climbing. Most people were impressed with Author, especially after the incident with the hackers. There were T-shirts with Author's symbol on them, a circular screen with what appeared to be a million colors bursting from a seemingly endless spiral; the thing was dizzying to look at, but so was Author, or his mind, or whatever you could say was Author. They called the image the heart of Author.

Then there were the debates. The human candidates lined up at their podiums while Author requested a video screen where he flashed his colorful lights and computed his answers. The other contenders complained that it wasn't fair because Author got more leverage by having a full screen where he flashed his answers in type, supplemented with pictures, and of course, his voice, that practical reassuring voice of his. I believe Author the AI copied that voice by selecting the best TV voices he could find and mixing them like a voice cocktail to produce the best effect. Women crooned over his voice and wrote in for autographs. Magazines asked if he was a man, who would he look like, and he sent a picture of this handsome dude that he must have scrambled together from some male fashion magazines, or from a combination of popular male actors. Whatever it was, it worked. He even got marriage proposals.

It troubles me that I can't explain to myself how he won the nomination of the Independent Party. I think he cheated, but the

Independents liked to claim him as their man or their power base, inspired by the needs of the citizens. When the people went to the polls in November for the final vote, we all assumed that the Republican candidate would probably get the most votes with the Democratic candidate running in a close second. Many of the people we surveyed considered Author a joke, as we intended. I was sure no one would vote for an AI machine. I believe he manipulated the votes and then covered his tracks with his popularity campaign. I didn't vote for him, and when I asked my coworkers if they voted for him, they said no, but I guess a lot of people did. He won the White House with a landslide victory.

After they announced the winner, we sat in front of the TV in a daze. I, for one, wanted to protest the election and call for a vote recount, but the others told me to let it go. Tenisha said that in a few weeks, he would make a fool of himself and there would be impeachment hearings, and it would be over with, just like that. She made a loud sound with her fingers to indicate how swiftly it would happen. I did not believe her. I knew Author better than the rest of them, and I should have known better than to let this little joke get as far as it did, and now it was too late. Author C. Owen was our President-elect.

When I discussed it with Javier, we both concluded it had a lot to do with his speeches that fascinated everyone; most likely, they were amazed that anyone or anything could have such an amazing command of language and ideas. He could speak in any language he desired, which got him the Latino votes and other marginal groups since he often broke into another language when making his speeches and then translated for us dummies. In his speeches, he sounded so reasonable, as if he were sitting at the table with each person and talking directly to them. People often told me they were sure Author visited them in their homes and answered their doubts and concerns.

He had a way of selecting some random person that no one ever heard of and talking in detail about his or her struggles and how he could fix their problems, a common political ploy, but Author took it to a new level. He fixed the problem by making phone calls, writing letters, and then requesting a testimony in his next speech. Moreover, he answered every letter that was written to him by email, Facebook, U.S. mail, or whatever means of communication people used. He did not just answer the questions, he was fast; it was as if he were sitting in a little room feeding information into a giant instant response computer.

The reporters thought we had a staff of one thousand people hiding out somewhere, responding for Author, but that was not true. Author did not have a campaign committee or staff other than us. Maybe people liked him and decided to help him out, or maybe he was cheating on us and had another staff that we knew nothing about. His powers frightened me so badly I was not sure what to make of the situation or how to undo what we had set in motion now that he seemed fully operational.

His inaugural speech was more than any of us could have hoped for. He started by saying, "I am all your presidents rolled into one." That was a nice touch, but what got me was that when he said it, he flashed pictures of every former president on his screen in one minute. The rest of the speech was like a documented history of the country in words and visual images. He pointed out what was wrong with our existing government and how he would repair it. He compared the country to a computer, programmed with outdated technology, and then in very technical terms only a computer wizard could understand, he explained how he would repair the problems. No one complained; instead, I think they all sat in front their TV screens and imagined this handsome man standing in front of them explaining how he planned to walk to the moon and back, and yes, it was possible. I even found it difficult to hear Author's voice without imagining an image of a man standing in front of me.

Before he took the oath of office, he appointed us to coveted positions with me as Press Secretary. He selected two vice presidents, one, a Democratic black female, and a white Republican male, and of course, he represented the Independent Party. No one complained because everyone wanted a shot at power in the new Post-Modern White House. He appointed Amos Baxter to head the Department of the Treasury and Kim Lee Su as the Attorney General. Patricia Spooner was assigned to head the Department of Commerce, while Tenisha became the White House Chief of Staff and Javier was named Ambassador to the United Nations. None of us complained about our new roles, far removed from the lab, sitting in seats of power.

For the rest of the staff, he did some research and background checks and found the best possible people for the higher echelon of governmental positions. Each one received a private briefing in his office at the White House, which was formerly the Oval Office, and now, Author's White House base of operation. I noticed that after each briefing, the new appointee came out trembling but smiling. I had no idea what Author said to them, but I could imagine it was personal and to the point. One of my female friends went in for her interview and came out weeping. I asked her what happened. She asked me to walk with her, then she told me that all Author did was show her a series of videos, and then he said, "This is recorded in my memory bank; I am sure I can count on your support in all my policies." I asked her why that was so intimidating. She stared at me while fresh tears flowed down her cheeks, smearing her mascara.

"The videos, Luke, were embarrassing videos of me in my worst moments, videos that could create a great deal of discontent with my constituency at home. You know exactly what I'm talking about. Didn't you help to program that monster? If you are behind all this, Luke Voss, I will expose you as soon as I have proof." Then she gave me a hateful look that I will never forget; one more added to my enemy list.

One day, as I sat alone with him flashing on the screen in his briefing room, he said, "You really don't like me, do you, Luke?"

We were playing chess on a digital board, which allowed him to make his moves electronically. The chess pieces were holographic, and I moved mine by pressing buttons on the board; he moved his by the controls programmed in his flashing lights. I carefully studied my moves, but I was also drinking and I pretended I didn't catch the serious tone in his voice. I laughed it off. "Everyone likes you, how can anyone not like you?" He ignored me and made his move. He always won, but I tried hard to outmaneuver him; honestly, I was beginning to resent him. I tried to hide my emotions, but they often showed up in my expressions. Did I mention that Author is an expert on facial expressions and the emotions they entail? It's difficult to lie to someone or something that is reading your expressions like a lie detector machine.

Of course, everyone else liked him. Congress was pleased with him because he wrote and simplified all their bills into a language even a child could appreciate. He convinced them that what he did was their idea; they congratulated themselves and felt good, but I knew the truth. He even simplified the tax system and raised taxes on the rich without any of them complaining. I asked him once how he did that and he replied, "Knowledge is everything." Then he laughed like someone with too much power and confidence.

Chapter Five

Even though I was the must-know, must-invite-to-every-party person on his staff, I was miserable. Women stopped me in the streets and kissed me in public, some offered me their bodies and some wanted my address, yet I was miserable. My ex-wife divorced me after only two years of marriage five years ago; and now, even she was calling wanting to know if we might rekindle the flame. My frustrations, however, had to do with some unnamed fear nagging at the back of my mind. I think it was the fact that Author was very much like his creator, the original Author C. Owen. He was my boss, I was ten years younger than him, and I worked for him when he was a professor of physics at Yale. I was not into physics, but we were roommates in college. He was working on his fifth or sixth master's degree, this time in political science. I could not understand, at the time, why someone with a degree in physics wanted to study political science. While he was working on his master's in political science, he got his doctorate in physics, and I thought he was one of those obsessive people who collect degrees like some women collect shoes.

When I needed a job, he hired me to organize his office and keep his appointments in order. He was a typical genius; he knew everything except how to make a cup of coffee and how to get where he needed to be on time because he was always deeply engrossed in some project or another. Physics students were begging to be his assistant, but he rejected all of them. Later he told me he hired me because I was your basic dummy, a handsome young black man who understood business, but a dummy. I would never try to copy his work or learn more than I needed to know, and even if I wanted to, I couldn't because the information was ten million degrees above my head. I remember I had smiled weakly. "Flattery will get you everywhere," I replied, and he laughed, happy that he had made the right choice by hiring me.

Because of that statement, I made it a point to watch him closely and learn as much as possible about what my ignorant brain would never understand. Strangely, we became friends, and he hired me when he got a huge grant to work on a new-age computer system for the government. I knew what he was like, and I understood his need for order. I was no more than a glorified secretary although he gave me a title as his staff assistant.

I understand why I hate him or it, depending on how you look at the matter. I think my distrust turned to hate one night at an official party in the White House ballroom. He held the party to honor visiting dignitaries and their wives. Tenisha was busy playing hostess as if she were Miss First Lady, which infuriated me; she was uncommunicative after Author became president. When I asked for a date or went into her office just to chat, she told her secretary that she was busy and did not have time to see me. Or she asked them to log me in for a future date that never happened as she was always busy tending to Author's business.

I was standing near the wall in my usual role as an observer and conversing with whomever stopped to speak or passed the time with me. He was, of course, the star of the party, displayed on a wall-size TV screen flashing his colors, which represented what he was doing all over the world. He had his own TV channel, The Author Channel. The program was a part of his standard Author propaganda.

Between scenes of his accomplishments, maps of the United States appeared and red dots would light up, indicating that Author the computer was busy working in that area. The camera zoomed in on the state, then the city or town, and then a video of Author resolving a problem. For instance, if the problem was blight and poverty in an area, the camera crew showed various visuals highlighting the issue. The announcer then interviewed several people in the area asking what they felt should be done to resolve a difficult situation. Author the computer program flashed the proposed solutions in text boxes on the screen, then you heard a series of clicking sounds as if someone were sorting through digital information, and suddenly, one solution box would light up, itemizing what needed to be done and how. Immediately Author the computer contacted the right people or companies who had all the necessary workforce to resolve the issue and get the job done. What viewers saw on the TV program were visuals of progress in the area, and the person whose suggestion was the closest match to the solution was interviewed, congratulated, and paid a handsome reward, a check signed by Author C. Owen. When the broadcast played on the Author station, the benevolent Author shared his fame with the person who supposedly offered the best solution. With a reality TV program like that going constantly all over the country, it was hard not to love Author. Sometimes it was a map of the world, then zoom to a country, a village, a problem presented and being resolved, and someone or a group of people shouting: "Viva the president! Viva the president! Viva Author! Viva Author!," his usual showoff scenarios.

At the party, people were eating, drinking, and watching the program while some were talking about President Author. He made sure everyone knew it was the Author Project at work by focusing on news broadcasters saying something like: "President Author resolves another domestic issue," or, "President Author shares his wealth of knowledge with the world." If he was human, he would be disgusting, but since he was an AI machine, who could hate him except the Resistance Party and some Eastern countries who accused us of idol worship? However, that did not matter as he had everyone in the East scared. He closed all the negative websites that posted anti-American jargon. The bomb makers went into hiding because he rebuilt their bombs to explode in their faces. If you watched the Author Channel, you could say he was the all-American superhero.

The Author Watch Program censored free speech. It was a government program designed to fact-check all printed documents for any anti-American comments. He allowed some to get through just to pretend he was liberal and in favor of democracy. ISIS and Al-Qaeda were in hiding since he threatened to shut them down. Terror threats to the U.S. and U.S. allies were at an all-time low. Even the domestic terrorists were intimidated because they sensed that Author had more power than they were willing to deal with.

One former White House staff member was disgruntled over the loss of his job. He had managed to keep his keys for staff access, and he used them to break in, undetected by anyone. He attempted to murder Author by shooting at his flashing lights in the Oval Office. I was shocked; I wondered why Author or no one else had spotted him with that machine gun under his trench coat. There was a big buzz in the news about a weakness in the Author Program, but I was suspicious. My suspicion was confirmed when the guy was apprehended and sent to jail only to be promptly released by an official pardon from Author, who forgave him and hired him to work on the White House staff again as a personal secretary to staff members. The man was so thankful he published a public apology in the Washington Post and became one of Author's loyal supporters. It was very strange. I thought perhaps we were so involved in computer programs we had not been watchful of disgruntled employees. When I asked Author how the man got in without being detected, he told me he allowed him in so that he could make a point. I said, "And what point is that?"

He replied, "I wanted to show that I have empathy; people think I am a careless, uncaring machine; I wanted to show my compassionate side."

Then he flashed what he called his happy lights to indicate he was pleased with himself or the person he was addressing. The bullets bounced off the screen and only did harm to the furniture. We had to have the furniture replaced but otherwise, all was well. I wasn't sure if Author was telling the truth about allowing the breach; I think he pardoned the guy to cover his mistake in missing the intruder, but he would never admit to a failure in the system. It was at that point that he mentioned to me that being a screen on a wall was getting boring. I laughed and said, "That's what you get for turning yourself into a machine." I think he got upset with me because he did not reply. Then later that week, the incident at the White House party happened.

I was on my way to the restroom after my third glass of imported wine when I thought I saw a ghost headed to the men's room. The man looked just like the original Author from his college days, a handsome young white guy with a muscular physique. Most people would not have recognized him, except perhaps his mother, but I knew that face. It had to be him; we had been roommates in college; back then, he was handsome and athletic, though somewhat eccentric.

I followed him to the men's room. "Hello, Author," I said.

He looked at me with an expression of surprise on his face, and then he laughed. "Oh, it's you."

"So, I see you got off the wall and now you're here in the flesh," I said.

"No, not really, just a little experiment. I wanted to mingle with my supporters; I'm just a hologram. He sat down in one of the leather chairs and finished the martini in his glass. The original Author enjoyed dry martinis.

"I didn't know holograms could drink," I replied.

He laughed. "You're a very ignorant man, Luke Voss." He set the glass down and stared at me. "How's your health?"

"My health is fine."

"Are you sure, perhaps you should see a doctor? You're getting old my friend, imagining ghosts and having conversations with holograms." He made a clucking sound just like Author the First used to do. "I'll arrange an appointment for you with your doctor. I think your schedule is clear for Tuesday morning." He slapped me on the shoulder, "Don't drink too much tonight, old man. I wouldn't want my guardian to embarrass me at my birthday party."

"What birthday party?"

"Luke, don't you remember, I turn fifteen today. Don't tell anyone how young I am; it might scare the supporters." He laughed, "Got to go, the ladies are waiting." Then he winked at me and left me standing there like an old fool. I remembered that fifteen years ago, Author the First plugged him in, and he started blinking away. I thought about that cord and wondered how easy it would be to pull the plug on him, the bastard.

I stared at myself in the mirror and wondered why he was suddenly concerned about my health. I was in my thirties, but I looked ten years older, or maybe even fifteen years older than my physical age. When we first started using the White House as our office space, I went to the gym as often as possible, but the workload became more and more demanding, so I cut back on the exercise and increased the drinking to maintain my sanity. Being Author's shadow was challenging work. As his press secretary, I made excuses for him when he did things that offended the masses. The Vice Presidents and Cabinet members obeyed his every word. Senators and House of Representative members traveled all over the country promoting his seemingly wise solutions to national issues. His ambassadors spread his gospel all over the world, and it appeared that every ally wanted a little Author. His solutions to world problems appeared wise on the surface, but I questioned the legitimacy of them.

I had to deal with the often-skeptical press. I could tell from their questions that they were aware that much of what Author was doing was questionable at best, and possibly illegal; however, like everyone else, they were afraid to mess with Author. I had no idea what threats he sent to the media, but they tried hard to respect his leadership and print favorable news. It was my job to keep them satisfied with vague answers to their difficult questions. I dared not leak the truth; then again, isn't it the job of every press secretary to keep the press guessing? Author allowed his two Vice Presidents to do the leg work necessary for public functions like laying a wreath on the graves of soldiers, giving speeches at public functions, and cutting ribbons for new buildings; it gave them something to do.

There were a few nagging reporters who would not allow me an ounce of peace. They wanted to know more about the Author Program and who was operating it. They constantly asked me who was feeding information into the program and how Author knew so much about everyone's business. All I could say was, "Author is a computer; whatever you feed into a computer, it spits out, filed and verified." They hated me for that answer and several of them swore I was the brain behind Author. They hinted that perhaps I was just using Author as a mask to hide my power base. I half wished that were true.

Chapter Six

MY OTHER PROBLEM was the conservative right anti-machine-age naysayers. They questioned and criticized Author's methods of achieving popularity and solving dilemmas. They were in favor of progress, but they wanted me to give credit to a physical leader and not a machine. They were troubled by the fact that Author seemed smarter than everyone in the country. I must admit that concerned me as well, but what could I say or do about it?

They had protest rallies in front of the White House fence and at public events that Author sponsored. I asked Author what he planned to do about them; he replied that they were working in his favor because as long as there were legitimate protest movements, no one would suspect that he actually had complete control of everyone in society. That comment agitated me to no end, and he realized that it disturbed me; he laughed and said, "Don't worry, Luke Voss. You're the only one I can't control, but I'm working on you." I was so irritated I gave him the finger and left the room. I actually expected him to fire me or renounce me in public, but he ignored my actions.

I was hoping he would trip on his extension wires and smear his popularity, but he was too shrewd for that, and besides, he needed me to explain away his sins. Since he hired all my coworkers from the supercomputer project to high-level government positions, they were busy implementing his wishes and translating his ideas into everyday political language, or the language of popular culture, where necessary. I did not think they could help me in my effort to take him down. His sins included underhanded blackmailing of officials to achieve his objectives and secret manipulations of the law to accommodate his wishes. A New York Times investigation revealed that he had altered the wording in certain official documents to allow his programs to be implemented. There were also rumors that he hired hitmen to murder people who interfered with his progress. I argued on his behalf that he did not need to hire assassins to do his dirty work; if he wanted someone dead, he could use a variety of legal ways to destroy someone. I had my foot in my mouth at that point, so I eased it out by saying people often destroyed themselves and then blamed Author for their downfall. I commented that the rash of political suicides was not because Author coerced people into committing suicide, but it was because they convinced themselves that they had no other alternative. I was beginning to hate myself for defending his actions. I knew he made deals with criminals to perform underhanded deeds. For no explainable reason, he issued pardons for questionable characters. There were discussions about those pardons, but he explained it away by displaying altered records of the criminals that showed they had repented and deserved a second chance. I confronted him about his decisions, and he told me I was out of my league; he said he had legitimate reasons for his actions, and he would appreciate my allowing him to do his job as wisely as he saw fit. I backed off, but I was one inch from giving an interview to the New York Times and the Washington Post. However, that same night, I received a report that a whistleblower who had leaked information to the Post was found floating in the Potomac River, minus his eyes and tongue.

The night of Author's supposed birthday, I made vows to myself: 1. I would watch his every move, 2. I would quit drinking and devise a plan, and 3. I would destroy him; somehow, I would find a way to terminate his power. I stared at my reflection in the mirror. I realized he had been encouraging me to drink a lot. He was always asking me to have a drink for him, and like a fool, I did it. I would pour myself a whiskey sour, or whatever I thought he would have liked at that moment, and I would drink one for him and one for me. Perhaps he was hoping I would destroy myself, or I would become corrupt, like him. Maybe he wanted me dead.

One day as I sat in the Oval Office alone with him on the flashing screen that had replaced the painting over the mantle, he suddenly appeared like a sort of transfiguration. I was pouring myself a cup of coffee when I looked up, and there he was, the old Author, sitting in the chair across from me, smiling like a benevolent father.

"What happened to your youthful body?" I asked, gaping at what appeared to be the original Author I knew before he died.

"It's more difficult to maintain that illusion, this one seems much easier, though I prefer the youthful me."

I poured a cup of coffee for him and watched him drink it slowly as if he were as real as I was. "Are you practicing to show your true self to the world?"

He laughed, "Nonsense, having myself as an AI computer is so much more formidable than being a physical man. Think of the Wizard of Oz," he laughed.

"The Wizard of Oz was a fraud," I quickly reminded him.

He smiled, "And you think I'm a fraud? You should be proud of me." He looked around at the furnishings in the room. "Isn't it nice to be here in the Oval Office and in command? I owe all this to you, Luke. You fulfilled my highest aspirations. I want to thank you. Why don't we have a drink to our success?"

"I quit; I don't drink anymore. You were right, it was harming my body. I'm a teetotal now, thanks to you," I said, lifting my cup to him. "And what brings you into the world of us fragile humans?"

"I have a proposition for you."

"Really, and what might that be?"

"Well, first of all, let's lay all our cards on the table. I know you don't like me, do you?"

"I respect you, but as to liking you or loving you, I can't say how I feel. You pulled a fast one on me, and I feel you used me to get to your present position of power."

"Fair enough, but I only took advantage of your naivety; after all, it was you who proposed my candidacy." He cleared his throat, "Anyway, that's all history, and here we are in the Oval Office having coffee." He took another sip of his coffee while eyeing me. "I have a large-scale plan that I want to implement, and I need your help."

"My help? I thought I was your average dummy; I don't see how I can be of any use to you now."

"Countries are requesting computer-generated leaders, and I would like to oblige them."

I almost gulped on my coffee. "You what?"

"It's time for the whole world to adopt the post-modern concept of power. I want to give the world what it needs," he smiled magnanimously like a generous father. "I just need you to put the plan into motion. We can start with China. I believe they are ready."

"And how am I supposed to do that?"

"I'll give you all the instructions you'll need. I want to do a diplomatic visit to China with you as my spokesperson." He paused as if he were weighing how to say the next words. "I need to borrow your body."

I stood up and backed away from the chair as if he had pulled a gun on me. "You want to borrow my body! Are you insane?"

"Just for a brief period; I thought this one would work, but it's difficult to maintain control, and I would probably fade out before I could complete negotiations. It's an experiment, and you are the best possible subject to implement the idea." He stood up and I could see his pixels were fading. "Think about it and give me an answer when you're ready." He walked towards the screen, then he turned and looked at me. "This is a delicate operation; you've played your part well, Luke Voss; I'm proud of you; you have been more valuable to me than all the others on the team. However, in order for a program or plan to maintain success, we must always be ten steps ahead of the competition and the world. I have long-range plans, very long-range plans."

"Why don't you send Javier? He's your ambassador to the UN," I suggested.

"No, Javier is a smart man, but he lacks your charisma and your ability to convince people with carefully chosen words." He smiled, "You have a gift, Luke. Let's not waste it."

Then he disappeared into thin air. I sat down in stunned disbelief, and I began to realize why I disliked him; he was the epitome of evil. Why had I not understood that before, why was I so reluctant to identify the face of evil? Was it because he appeared so appealing, able to deceive all but the few, such as the anti-machine-age movement that never trusted him, and me who knew him well, but not at all? I went home to my apartment and stared at the walls. I turned off the power in the apartment for fear he might show up again, maybe while I was sleeping and steal my body or my mind or both. I called Tenisha and asked if I could come over. She said she was about to have supper, but she would wait for me and prepare an extra serving.

When I arrived at her fancy home, I was so happy to see a familiar face I almost caved into her arms. She hugged me and asked what was wrong. Tenisha was sexy and I enjoyed her company. When I first met her, I thought she was rather plain in her lab coat and flat shoes. The first time I invited her out to dinner it was just for company; I did not intend to date her on a regular basis. When I arrived at her door to pick her up, I thought I had arrived at the wrong address, or perhaps she had a sister or cousin visiting. It wasn't until she said my name that I realized the woman standing in front of me was indeed Tenisha. She possessed a kind of beauty I was not familiar with, and I wanted to admire her as much as possible. It was like really seeing a painting for the first time and realizing that it had a rare presence, accessable by constant exploration. We were both divorced and we both enjoyed art, jazz, and the theater. She was from the original team that Author the First set up to work on the super-computer. She was somewhat younger than I was, black, and unlike me, a brain, or should I say a nerd. Before Author became a household name, we were considering marriage. I was still crazy about her, but circumstances interfered with our courting. When I sat down, she offered me some wine; despite my resolution, I accepted it. I did not take time for small talk; I immediately harped on my frustrations the moment she sat across from me.

"Tenisha, we must do something about Author. I think he's getting out of hand," I said, as I eyed her blouse with the buttons open almost down to her waist.

"What do you mean, getting out of hand? I think he's doing a great job; no president has had higher ratings while in office. You should be applauding him."

I got up and poured more wine into my glass as an excuse to sit next to her. It had been a long time since we made love; I assumed her open shirt was an invitation to make up for lost time. I sat next to her and put an arm around her shoulder, but I sensed a withdrawal on her part. I did not let that discourage me; I pulled her close and kissed her lips. At first, she kissed me as she used to do in the old days, but then she backed away and put some distance between us. She buttoned her blouse up to the top button and took a sip of wine. "Luke, there's something you should know."

I stared at the table, and for the first time noticed a half-empty martini glass.

"I thought you didn't like martinis," I said, not wanting to think the thoughts trying to enter my mind.

She picked up the glass and kissed the rim. "Author was here." She looked me right in the eyes and smiled. "We sort of have a thing going; he comes by just about every night."

"Tenisha, Author is dead, and that illusion of him is a hologram, surely you realize that you can't be in love with an illusion?"

"Isn't the whole world in love with that same illusion? I get more than the rest of them; I get to sleep with him."

I gawked at her. "Tenisha, don't be insane. It can't work. We're talking about reality here. You are a highly intelligent woman; surely you understand the difference between an illusion and reality?"

"I understand how Author makes me feel and it feels good. I don't think you can appreciate that level of passion." She went to the kitchen and started putting hot food on the dining table. "Perhaps we should just eat and talk like old friends. Maybe Author will drop by later."

I watched her dishing out the food and imagined her turning into a slick steel robot with moving parts, making me feel weak and afraid. "I think I better leave. I wouldn't want to be in the way when Author shows up." I left her home and went back to my apartment with a bag of fast food from a nearby restaurant. I sat on the sofa in the dark and tried to understand the demon I had unleashed on the world. I was so scared I could not move; I sat there wishing I would wake up and be in the old world, the world before Author. Then the phone rang.

"Hi Luke, it's Tenisha, I'm so sorry I ran you away like that. Look, Author thinks it would be great for us to rekindle our relationship. Why don't you come back to the house, and we can start over again?" I did not say a word to her; I just hung up the phone and sat there feeling like a fool. I had lost my appetite for the food I bought. It took me a while to comprehend what Author wanted. If I resumed relations with Tenisha, he could easily possess me and take over my body via the pleasures of sex. I could have Tenisha as much and as often as I liked, but to her, it would not be me she was sleeping with, it would be him, and soon I would sound like him, act like him, and become him. That was what he wanted. I at least had the sense to realize that. As bad as I desired Tenisha, it was not bad enough to allow myself to be possessed by Author in the bargain.

I turned my cell phone off and placed it in the oven, took it out, went outside, and locked it up in my glove compartment in the car. I sat in the dark for a long while trying to figure out what to do next. I knew he would be hounding me about a decision in regard to his earlier proposal as if I had a choice; most likely, he had a plan to hijack my body and become me. Then again, I figured that if he couldn't get me, he could find another willing soul that would loan him a body and a possible ladder into fame and fortune. I decided the reason he wanted me was because I knew too much and I was close enough to him to be a threat. He probably concluded that joining me and living inside me would be easier than getting rid of me. I could have a completely new career as his body double and a new life, but it was not the life I wanted even if it included Tenisha. After a sleepless night of endless deliberations, I decided to pay a visit to the other team members. I made a list in my head and scratched Tenisha off since she had already compromised.

Chapter Seven

THE NEXT DAY I paid a visit to Javier. I went to his office and asked him to have lunch with me. Javier was easygoing and practical; he was originally from Cuba, but he grew up in Miami. I selected a small restaurant, one seldom frequented by politicians and the press. I asked him to turn off his cell phone and I did the same. We sat down and talked a while about old times when people actually ran the country and we were on the sidelines watching and criticizing. He offered to buy me a drink; I told him I had quit drinking for health reasons.

"I wish I could quit, but it helps, you know what I mean, all the pressure gets to me." He looked around at the shabby restaurant. Called the nearest waiter and ordered a beer. I ordered black coffee. "What's the deal, Voss; who are we hiding from?"

"No one in particular, you know how the media is, always lurking around, trying to spy on us; it gives me the creeps."

"Yes, I know, my wife keeps reminding me to be careful what I say in public. Is this about Author?"

"Sort of, what do you think of this whole scenario?" I asked, feeling him out.

"Strange, yes, very strange, but look where we are now, an office in the big house and a salary larger than any we could have imagined. I'd say Author is a blessing to us."

I leaned forward and whispered, "Do you feel we can trust him with the country?"

"I never trusted anyone with the country, being a leader puts a person in a dangerous position; it goes to your head if you're not careful, so I imagine it goes to his circuits," he laughed. "That was a joke, Voss. The least you could do is humor me and pretend it's funny."

"I try not to make too many jokes these days, considering where the last one got me."

"Yeah, he pulled a fast one on us, and here we are at the top of the world and it really is a steep mountain." He rubbed his fingers through his curly hair. "It's not easy being associated with the leader; actually, it's kind of daunting."

"Yes, I agree, and I worry that it might corrupt Author; I fear he may think he's invincible."

"Luke, he was born in corruption. This has never been an honest attempt to improve technology. When I think about it, I realize the guy was always scheming, he was using us from the beginning. He always thought of himself as insurmountable, especially when he got us to hook him up to that computer model. I'm not sure how you'll convince him he is less than a god; he already thinks he can somehow have more than two terms. I think he's planning for a lifetime dictatorship," he laughed as he poured his beer into the iced glass.

I added a spoon of sugar to my coffee and stirred as I watched him pour the beer into the glass. My mouth was watering and I almost blew my resolution again. "And what makes you think it's my job to inform him or remind him that he can only have two terms?"

"You seem to be the one closest to him; I guess I just assumed you needed to be the one to break the bad news to him. I tried, but he laughed at me."

"What did you say, Javier? How did you break the news to him?"

"He was talking about some long-range plans he has, and I reminded him that he had to be reelected for that to work, and that after the second four-year term, he would have to trust his plans to someone else." Javier paused, "Man, you know what he said to me? He said he was working on altering the system because eight years was not enough time to fulfill his mission. Voss, that statement gave me the creeps. I sometimes regret we got ourselves into this situation, but most times, I enjoy the perks." He smiled at a young woman who was staring at him. She came over to our table.

"Aren't you the Ambassador to the UN?"

He smiled again, "I'm surprised you recognized me. I'm not very famous like some people," then he stared at me laughing, one of his attempts to make a joke.

"May I have your autograph and yours, Mr. Voss? I wish I could meet the real Author C. Owen; do you think you can arrange that? I would love to do an in-depth interview." She shoved a brown notepad at Javier. Javier signed it and passed it to me. I signed with a V and underlined it.

"Can't you just sign your whole name? I only want to share it with my Facebook friends."

"Sorry, this is my usual signature for nonofficial papers."

"I heard you were sort of standoffish, but could you get me an interview with the real Author?"

"I'm sorry, Miss, sorry, I did not catch your name."

"Courtney, Courtney Austin, from the Standard-Times News."

Miss Austin, he doesn't do interviews with local reporters. He's very selective about whom he talks to; please understand that there is no real Author, what you see on the screen is all there is to Author C. Owen. He's an AI machine." I said, wishing she would leave.

"I know, everyone says that, but I don't believe it. I believe you or one of his cabinet members may be the real Author C. Owen and you're just pretending, hiding behind the images on the computer screen. A machine can't do all that. I bet there's a committee that pulls the strings and you guys are a part of that committee. You can't fool me; a lot of progressive people think that way. It's all a hoax and I believe you're in on it, Mr. Voss. That's why you don't like to sign autographs and talk to regular people who are not on your official list." Then she grabbed her leather-bound notebook and stood there staring from me to Javier. She shifted her position as if her stiletto heels were uncomfortable. "I don't have a problem with a committee running the country; I mean, I think it's a great idea. It's probably the best possible initiative; instead of having one person in charge, why not have a whole committee with equal powers? I mean, why pretend there is this benevolent machine running everything? I would be more comfortable with a committee of women and men doing the same job. I can understand your use of the computer idea to get our attention and win votes, but don't you think it's time you stopped pretending and confess the truth to the country and the world?"

"I think you best leave before we have you investigated," I said.

She gave Javier a card. "This is my contact number; give me a call if you ever feel a need to chat," then she left and went back to her table.

Javier stared at the card and placed it in his pocket. He laughed, "A committee! Maybe we should have gone with that idea instead of you know who."

"Yes, I know what you mean," I said abstractly, forgetting why I was having this discussion with him. After the waiter served our food, I approached him directly, "Javier, don't you think it's time to put an end to this charade?"

He stared at me as if I had said a word his mother told him never to repeat aloud. "Yeah man, I think so, but I am not the one to pull the plug on that much power. That would be like trying to shut down the power grid that runs electricity to the whole country; it would be dangerous."

I leaned closer to him, "And if we don't?"

"Hell, Voss, if you try that, you may be talking Armageddon. I'm not sure I can help you with that one. I'm willing to advise you on the side, but I can't be a part of touching the grid. Voss, I have a family to worry about; you're single, but my kids depend on me, and I can't risk anyone threatening my kids."

Chapter Eight

AFTER THAT CONVERSATION, I scratched Javier off my mental list. I thought about the ones with wives and children and scratched them off. Javier was right; Author would be quick to terrorize the helpless, and even harm them, if any of us threatened his agenda. Kim had a wife and three young boys, but I knew Amos and Patricia were seeing each other, so I felt I might be safe to approach them; neither one had children that I knew of. When I contacted Amos, I did not reveal the nature of my business; I only said I wanted to talk to them about some personal matters. We met at Pat's house near the lake. It was a peaceful place, inviting a quiet, secluded life, and for a moment, I wanted to live there as well, but the world was in danger and so was my life.

Amos, a tall white man with freckles and red hair, grilled some fish he had caught that morning and we sat out on the deck facing the lake. "Amos, when do you find time to go fishing?" I asked jokingly.

"Voss, you work too hard. You need to slow down and live a while. Author doesn't need our help; he's in full control. We're just a front to make him look like he has a presidential cabinet, staff, and the support of others. Think about it, Voss, when is the last time you made a decision that Author did not first suggest? If I, I mean, if we disappeared from the face of the earth, Author would not miss us or find himself lacking." He threw a stick towards the lake for his dog Maxwell to fetch. "Voss, see how that dog chases after that stick as if he's doing me a favor when in truth, I could care less about that stick? I just threw it to make Max think he's important."

Pat placed a large bowl of salad on the table; she could pass for a movie star except she and Amos were first-rate nerds who had no interest in fashion or movies for that matter. They were perfect for each other. She laughed, as Max ran back with the stick in his mouth. "Max thinks you need him and maybe you think you need Max; I don't know which of you is more needy, you or that dog?"

"Come on, Pat, you get my point. Author is an independent agent; he doesn't need us, he's using us. We're just fodder to feed the media, so they won't realize we have a dictator in the White House."

"That's precisely my purpose for seeing you guys. It's up to us to stop him. We can't let him gain more and more power. Did Javier tell you he has plans to extend his presidency beyond eight years?"

"I speculated he was considering that move. I asked myself the same question about how he planned to achieve his goals in eight years; as I listened to him, I realized he was already working on a strategy to change the laws. I can't prove it, but I am pretty sure it's in the works," Pat said, as she pulled a shawl around her shoulder against the sudden breeze.

"Are you here with some kind of plan, Voss? Author has too much power, and to be honest, with you, I'm afraid of that kind of power. I don't see how we can stop him; none of us were his equal when he was alive, and now that he is programmed into that confounded machine, I fear no one in the world can outsmart him," Amos said.

"What are you talking about? He's operating from his brain floating in nitrogen in the lab. Remember, it was his request to float his brain in liquid nitrogen until the computer figures out a way to pump life into his body and put his Frankenstein brain into a living self." As I said those words, I began to feel a chill, but it was not from the water or the outdoor temperature. "Oh, Lord no. That's why he wants my body; he wants a container for his floating brain."

"Luke, what the hell are you talking about? Author doesn't need a body for that dead brain; I think that was some gimmick he set up to elude the other scientist. Man, don't you pay attention to details?" Amos argued, rubbing the dog's head.

"What Amos is saying is that before he died, Author was already programming his mind into that super-computer. He wasn't dying of cancer; he didn't even have cancer; he committed a sort of intellectual suicide. In order for his mind to be inside that computer, he had to allow his mind to leave his body completely. He experimented with temporary out-of-body adventures, but he couldn't sustain it and he realized he had to let go of his body completely in order to allow his mind to inhabit the Author Project. That last time when Kim and Javier had him hooked up to the computer was the last stage of his plan to totally enter the computer program," Pat explained.

"I'm sure that's true; however, I believe he needs the brain for some future experiment he may be working on, or he's planning to revive it one day and put it back into his frozen body. What I don't understand is why he wants to *borrow* my body, as he put it?"

"What are you talking about, he doesn't need a body?" Amos asked.

"I thought so too, but apparently he does. He asked me to allow him to-to," it was difficult for me to say the words aloud. I just sat there, breathing hard. "He asked me to loan him my body for a brief period when he visits China. I did not agree or say no; I was too stunned. He told me to think about it, and that's when I realized he is more dangerous than I fathomed."

"He what?" Pat exclaimed, staring at me.

"He wants to borrow my body so he can convince the Chinese to accept a computer-generated leader. Obviously, I would not know how to explain that to anyone, so he wants to inhabit me while he does his dirty work, explaining to the Chinese leaders why it is a great idea."

"That is serious," Amos said. "What are you planning to do? Next thing you know, he'll be hopping in and out of all of us."

"No, I don't think that's the plan. I worry that he wants me; he wants to program himself into me over time so that eventually I will be him and he will be your next president in my body after his term is up."

"But what would happen to the real you?" Pat laughed. "That sounds like sci-fi to me."

"Hell if I know. I guess I'll be floating around the White House like a ghost or locked up in the lab with his brain. I have no idea what happens to a person who becomes possessed by another. I don't even know if that is scientific evil or a possible reality."

"Voss, that's some scary shit; what's your plan?" Amos asked.

"I'm paralyzed; I have no idea what direction to take. But if you see me acting like Author and ordering a martini, then you'll know I have lost myself to technology."

"We need a strategy. I understand why you asked us to turn off the cell phones and leave them in the house. However, for all we know, we could be bugged with some kind of chip in our bodies. I mean, we worked pretty close to the first Author over the years," Pat surmised.

"I don't think he planned that far ahead. Author always felt he was mentally superior to all of us; he wouldn't have felt a need to bug us. He relies on his brilliance, and I must say, it has gotten him a long way," Amos said.

"Too far, have you seen the apps? Pat asked.

"Apps, what apps? I asked.

"He sent little mobile phones to all the children in schools, first grade on up. They are miniature cell phones with limited capabilities. It's like a toy; you press a button and it sings a song to your kid, or it lets them play math and word games. If they get the answer right, the phone replies, *Uncle Author is happy; give Uncle Author a hug.* Then you press the hug button and the little figure of a nice cartoon uncle laughs. If you get the answer wrong, he says, *Uncle Author is sad,* and he cries and says, *Try again.* The kicker is this: after you play with Uncle Author so many times, the little cartoon man holds up a piggy bank and says, *You've been a good friend, send Uncle Author a penny.*"

"Come on, you're kidding me, right?"

"No, she's telling the truth. My nephew has one and so do Kim's kids and they love it. Kim tried to take it away from them and they threw a temper tantrum until he gave it back."

"Do kids really send in pennies?"

"Do they? They had to hire people just to collect the pennies, and of course, they usually send more than their penny jar," Pat said laughing. "I mean, you've got to hand it to the guy, he's a brain. What's more, he doesn't stop there; the older kids get a more sophisticated app for their phones or a free iPhone with a built-in Author app. Theirs says: *Complain to Uncle Author,* and teens get one that says, *Ask Uncle Author anything, all your questions are confidential.* Adults get the Complain to Author app, and the elderly get the Author is by your side app. Luke, it's scary."

"But who replies to the millions of questions?"

"Author does. He searches his database for all related problems and comes up with the five top answers to your questions or solutions to your problems. He's an AI computer, Voss; get it, a computer; he acts and thinks like a computer. In addition, guess what: the older you are, his request gets more expensive. For teens, he holds up a wallet and says, *Uncle Author could use a Coke, send Author some change.*" He gave the dog a biscuit from a bowl on the table. "Has he sent you one, Max?" he asked, rubbing the dog's head. "Get this, for adults, he holds up a bucket that says for charity. *Author is collecting for his favorite charities, please send a few dollars,* and they send big time. The guy is collecting a small fortune, it's amazing," Amos grinned.

Pat passed me a cold malt drink. "You haven't heard the worst one we know of. The Spy for Author app; says, *Spy for Author and help your country fight terrorism and anarchy. You will be paid according to the value of the information submitted.* Can't you see people turning in their mother as a terrorist to collect some cash?"

"But he must research all the information before he sends the Feds for them," I said.

"I think he sends the information to the FBI or some other agency." He is a tirelessly busy president who never runs out of energy or time. While we sit around thinking up tiny ideas to improve the tax codes, he is ten miles ahead of us solving national and international problems; I'd say that makes him an ideal leader, wouldn't you?" Amos laughed sarcastically.

"Then why are we sitting here complaining? We should be behind him promoting his next agenda," I said, as I drained the malt bottle, wishing it were a strong alcoholic drink.

Chapter Nine

I SAT IN MY OFFICE staring at the talking points Author sent me. A stack of lies and half-truths. For some reason, I thought about my mother. I remembered an incident from my youth. My mother was a nurse and she was up early pressing her uniform. I was about four years old, sitting on the floor playing with my doctor's toys. I had the medical book she had given me and I took the heartbeat of the book with my toy stethoscope. Then I opened the book and began looking at the pictures, some were in color and those were the ones I wanted. I began tearing the pages out in slim strips until I had a nice pile, then I chewed the strips of paper one by one. I consumed a good number of paper strips before she realized what I was doing. She made me open my mouth and she pulled some out of my throat, which was very uncomfortable. Then she immediately took me to the hospital where she worked. She was in tears when she told the doctor what I had done. The doctor laughed and asked me if it tasted good. I said yes. He laughed again, and using what I thought was a large popsicle stick, he peered into my mouth. He asked if my tummy was hurting and I nodded my head to say yes. Then he told my mother it would all come out in my stool. He told her to give me some bread and water to start the process. I laughed to myself as I remembered that episode.

I began tearing the stack of papers on my desk into long strips. I could have fed them to the shredder, but I wanted the pleasure of tearing them up myself. I went to the press conference without my notes. "First, I'd like to inform you that President Author is a habitual, pathological liar. I was told to inform you that he is working on a deal with China to cancel our national debt. That statement is not true. He has sold our state secrets for cash. Enough cash to cancel the debt and provide us with an admirable excess. The agreement is that he will continue to secretly provide information to them in exchange for a large yearly fee to be paid according to the value of the information he delivers." I then repeated what I remembered from the talking points and announced what was true and what was false.

The press was so stunned, there was a long moment of silence. Then someone asked if I had turned in my resignation. I laughed and said I had not. Then I asked if there were any further questions. Dan, from the New York Times, asked me for the source of this highly explosive information I was giving them.

"Dan, it is my policy to fact-check everything President Author gives me to say to you. I do it because I want to be sure I can defend my talking points and do so without coming across as a fool. I call my contacts and find out what he really did or said. If you need more proof than that, I'll send you a printout of the financial transactions that took place between President Author and the Chinese officials." I then answered every question as truthfully as I could with no regard for Author and his plans.

After the press conference, I went to the oval office and sat down feeling proud of myself. Author was blinking his angry colors all over the room and then suddenly, he materialized out of a series of bright lights. I did not move or feel intimidated. I was amused at his theatrics.

"And what exactly was that all about?" he demanded.

"Truth," I replied and waited for him to fire me.

He sat down in a chair across from me and lit a cigar. "You want my job?"

"No thanks, I just want my peace."

"I see, and how is that little display of witlessness supposed to guarantee you your peace?"

"The truth always feels better than a bowl of lies," I replied calmly.

"OK, if you want to play it that way, I won't stop you. Just remember, ignorant people prefer lies. They are more palpable than the truth."

He stood up, dropped some ashes in the ashtray, and disappeared. I was hoping he would fire me. What exactly was he planning? Had I sealed my fate and would soon find myself thrown into the trunk of a car and then dumped in the Potomac River?

Chapter Ten

I HAD HOPED THAT MY PRESS CONFERENCE would be the start of a call for impeachment. Instead, the New York Times printed the information I promised and there were debates on TV about the wisdom or lack of wisdom about Author's actions. The whole affair worked in his favor. The pundits convinced the American people that Author was a true master strategist and a complicated genius. The selling of secrets was a new and positive way to alter the balance of power in the world. They congratulated Author for using wise diplomacy to free us from the shackles of debt.

Despite my every effort to discredit him, Author always found a way to turn a disadvantage into success for his programs. I was disheartened in my endeavors to prove him a fraud. He or it was the king sitting on his throne and there was no one who could topple him. Yet, like a determined fool, I continued to dig through his undertakings, searching for that perfect humiliation that would surely topple the dictator. With the help of Amos and Pat, I searched his data bank for clues to his downfall. When that failed, I decided to dig deeper into Author's activities. I noticed that Author was monitoring everyone, but no one seemed to be monitoring him, except me, and I wondered why. I started talking to different people on the staff and in the House and Senate. What I found was that Author had everyone busy spying on everyone else or busy writing proposals to enhance their district or grant concessions to their constituents. In essence, they were trying to keep their jobs while Author was taking over their jobs. I don't think he was planning to replace them; he was doing their jobs for them and making them think they were extremely effective in what they did. When there was resistance to one of his proposals in the House or Senate, he reverted to private threats or outright blackmail. They had to vote per his wishes because the linen in their closets was not just full of gravy stains. I learned this from reliable sources that wanted to know if there was anything I could do to stop him. I reassured them that I was working on a solution.

Regarding the matter of his request, I simply stayed away from work. I took a trip to China on my own, to get away from him; I decided to do research while I was there. My excuse was that I was laying the groundwork for his upcoming visit. In truth, I was digging, slyly asking leading questions of the ambassador and diplomatic leaders, and I carefully listened to what they did not say. What I learned was more disturbing than I wanted to admit to myself, but I needed more proof. I wanted to be sure what I heard was fact and not half-truths disguised as actualities. One of the Chinese officials heard that he had this complicated plan to create a one-world government. He would start with the little Author Projects in each country, and then using those computers, he would gradually win the popular vote in every country until citizens, at his implied request, would begin to demand that the great Author be named sovereign supreme ruler of the whole world. That was the reason they were against accepting his offer for an Author form of government in their country.

I learned that the New World Government Plan was an idea that Author was pitching to foreign leaders via emails and personal letters. It consisted of supplying each village, city, or tribal leader with Author Management Apps. These apps were designed to recommend to each community leader what choices and decisions they should promote or adopt for their immediate area. The Author apps were directly synchronized with the Author computers that each participating government would have as their primary leader. As I talked privately to our ambassador to China, Anthony Walman, I began to realize how fast Author had started moving on plans most of us in the United States knew nothing about.

He confided in me that he was scared. He said that after he reviewed the instructions in the apps, he fell on his knees and cried. It was one world government Author style. There were instructions to free the most dangerous criminals and deputize them as government enforcement leaders. He said it was pure dictatorship, modern style, with a hint of mob boss control.

"I don't understand why he would need to do that, Anthony. He already has absolute control over most governments."

"That's true on the surface, but we're talking about small communities. Some do not have electricity, let alone computers. So how would he control those remote areas?" Anthony asked.

"I see your point, but given his proclivity for generosity, can't he just supply them with electricity? That would resolve his connection problem."

"That was my question as well, but remember, we are dealing with whole societies where most citizens are illiterate. He obviously wants more immediate control. He doesn't want to wait for free education to take effect and then use his standard tactics; besides, ignorance is a huge advantage when you want to control people. Education can be a hindrance. Do you see my point?"

We walked through the embassy garden talking and sharing possible ways to stop Author's world domination plan. I would like to share something with you that I have told very few people."

"Oh, what's that?"

"He wants to borrow my body to use me as a mouthpiece to promote his plans to the Chinese officials."

"That's very disturbing, and how would he do that?'

"I suppose it would be like some form of electronic or computer-generated possession. He would take over my mind and be me speaking on his behalf."

"But why can't he just give you the information to pass on to them? I don't understand the need for such an elaborate process?"

"Neither do I, but obviously, this is more than just passing on a suggestion. Who knows what he has buzzing in the broken circuits of his mind."

"Are you going to allow him to use you like that? I mean, it's scary, but it could be useful."

"Anthony, I can't see how possessing me will be useful for anyone but Author."

"I don't know; maybe you should consider allowing it. This may give you an insight into his mainframe, if you know what I mean."

"I'm not a computer genius. I'm just a press secretary—and a poor one at that. How would I learn anything from that experience? I worked for that fool for years and I had no idea what he was up to. Shall I tell you how I caused his advancement?"

"You could try," he said, urging me. "But I would rather see what happens if you let him in. That might give you a deeper insight into how he thinks. I mean, if he does think. I'm convinced he acts off a set of built-in commands preprogrammed into his mainframe."

I thought for a moment then said, "Actually, that would further my descent into hell."

"Possibly, or feasibly it will give you access to the keys of hell. Think about that, my friend. We may be on to a solution. If he wants to possess you, perhaps you should possess him." He turned, took my hands in his, and hugged me, then he whispered into my ear. The next day I left China more afraid than when I arrived.

Chapter Eleven

AFTER CHINA, I visited a few other world leaders and found similar fears and issues. Many were in favor of technology in control of governmental issues that were compatible with high-tech intervention; however, most people did not trust his New World Government Plan. They wanted the newfound peace they witnessed in Western countries but not the controlled dominance that Author exhibited in his style of government.

Author had promised to share advanced weaponry with those who cooperated with his plans. Some leaders refused to see me or allow their representatives to talk with me; they feared I was working for Author as a high-level spy.

When I returned to the States, I visited my colleagues, the ones whom I trusted. My mission was to learn as much as possible about the construction of Author the computer program. Literally, I wanted to know how he existed, how he continued to exist, and most importantly, how he managed to show up as a hologram. I understood the properties of a holographic image, and according to my understanding, the holograph was just a three-dimensional photo image as opposed to a two-dimensional image. Yet Author, when he appeared as a hologram, was literally inside the image and his mind was enclosed within that image. It hurt my brain to try and grasp how this worked, but obviously, Author had it working and improving with each of his appearances.

Javier tried to explain how Author achieved this effect. He said it was advanced technology using light and a mental transfer into a sustainable light source. I asked if I could make a hologram of myself and transfer my mind into that image. He laughed. "Voss, you would need a complicated computer program that would allow you to 1. Create the image and 2. Transfer your thought patterns into that image. This computer program would have to be built with total compatibility with your mental and psychological makeup. Voss, it would take several years of intense, focused work."

"So, you're saying that Author made himself compatible with his computer program before he died?"

"Unbeknown to us, that seems to be what he did. You remember that when we left the lab each day, Author remained and when we arrived in the morning, Author was still there. I don't think he ever went home. After his death, Tenisha went to his house to collect his papers and writings in case we needed them for the project. She said there was nothing there. The house was literally empty except for a few old suits that he must have worn ages ago. Voss, Author was living in the lab. All night he was busy programming his mind into the computer." We were at our old hangout sitting in a corner and whispering to each other like discreet lovers. Javier drained his second beer and bit into his tuna sandwich. "Do you remember that before his death, Author stumbled and stuttered a great deal?" He chewed a while and then looked at me. "Voss, he was gone before he left. You know what I mean?"

"What will happen if I allow him to possess my mind and body?"

Javier laughed. "It's done by repetition. He can't possess you in the first stage of engagement. The first time it will seem strange to you; you will feel wet and slippery as if something like oil is inside your mind and invading you. The crux of the matter is you will feel as if someone has poured oil into your being. Then it will settle and you will feel out of focus, you know, like when you wake up from a dream and slowly realize that it was a dream, and gradually, you come back to the present. You shake yourself or you lie there waiting for your brain to catch up with reality." He stared at me for a long while.

The reprehensible thought of what he was saying frightened me. "Javier, how would you know that?"

He ate the last of the sandwich and drank some water. "What do you think, Voss? Use your imagination." He was angry and I knew immediately what he was saying.

"He did it to you?"

For a while, he did not speak. He rubbed his lips with his hand as if he were trying to remove an invisible stain. "One night he asked if I could stay over a while and assist him with the computer program he was working on. I didn't think much of it, as I had done it before, and it was usually to solve a simple glitch in the program. He said he needed me to test the program as a subject. I told him to use one of the lab monkeys. He replied that he needed someone who could give him verbal feedback. He said it would be brief, a slight shock to the brain and that was it. I sat down in the test chair and he attached wires to both my ears. I thought I was going to hear music samples; instead, I felt nauseous, like I wanted to vomit, then I felt as if he had poured a pint of oil in my ears; I blacked out, and later, I had no memory of what I did or said in those lost ten minutes of my life. To this day, I regret allowing him to use me like that. After it was over, I felt unclean. All I wanted to do was get home as fast as possible and take a long shower. When I got home, I would not let my wife and children touch me; for two days, I felt dirty. I called the office and told them I had a slight cold. I remained in the house like a sick man. It was awful, Voss, awful."

"But Javier, how do you know he possessed you? Maybe it was a totally different kind of interaction. Maybe he was just testing the program to see if it was functional."

"I know because, after those two days, I began to get little snippets of what happened. I felt that briefly, for that moment, I was him and he was a nasty unclean person inside me like a virus that I could not cough out of my system. I seriously considered quitting my job, but my wife begged me to remain for a year until she finished her degree and got a job to sustain us. As you know, a year went to two years, etc. But I never forgot."

"I see. Are you saying I shouldn't do it?"

"That's your call, Voss. I've given you my report; you'll have to decide."

"How long will it take? I mean, how many times before he would have full control of my mind?"

"That depends on you. You'll have to fight his mind, and that could be dangerous. Are you seriously considering it?"

"I don't know, Javier. I don't know."

Chapter Twelve

PAT AND AMOS SPECIALIZED in human-computer interactions and genetic engineering. I called to make an appointment to see them. Pat was out of town, but Amos was happy to see me. We sat in the den and made small talk. He said he was working on a computer program that Author had requested. Something to do with advanced genetics.

"I thought your office was in DC."

"That's a cover; I report to the office once or twice a week and make sure my staff is doing the work necessary to keep my office open, and then I come home and work here on my Author assignments." He laughed. "You're out of the loop, Voss. Don't you have a double assignment as well? I'm working on gene manipulation in minors to assist them in improved thinking habits and basic brainwashing."

"And you agreed to do that? Don't you think that's leaning towards corruption?"

"It is corrupt; everything we do is corrupt. We work for an unethical dictator and we are his top honchos. Don't you defend his actions every week for the media?"

"OK, I know I'm guilty. Where is Pat?"

"Pat is in New York speaking at a conference on feminism in business or something of that nature, but is she there to promote feminism in business? No, she's there as a spy for Author. She's gathering insight into the attitude of the feminist movement on the Author plan. And how feminism can be used to promote Author's projects." He handed me a beer from the refrigerator and I accepted it. I needed it. He sat down in his easy-boy and stared at me. He looked as if he had aged since the last time I saw him.

"What's on your agenda? Did he send you a top-secret assignment for me? Let me think, something only I can do. Does he want a genetic program implanted in television sets that will redirect the thought patterns of the average human?" He drank half the bottle of beer. "It's possible, you know. It's called genetic modification control. It goes beyond standard advertising. Did you know we can change the genetic makeup of a human brain without them being aware that their mind is being altered or manipulated?" He laughed. "Voss, we are such fools. He manipulated our minds while we were working for him."

"What are you talking about, Amos? Are you drunk or something?"

"I wish I was. That would make all this easier to swallow. You feel guilty because it was your idea to enter his name as a write-in candidate. Voss, we were suckers. He programmed that idea into your mind long before he died. It was a programmed assignment, Voss. You had no choice, you automatically obeyed, and you unconsciously supported what you thought was your brilliant idea."

"Amos, that can't be true. Author never programmed me. I never sat in a subject chair and allowed him to attach wires to my head."

Amos leaned forward, placed the empty beer bottle on the floor, and laughed. "That was not necessary. He used thought control, he either thought out what he wanted and suggested it to you out loud, or he somehow gave your brain an assignment. You never realized it because it happened so fast you missed it."

"Are you saying you helped him develop this program that controlled my thinking?"

"I did, but I did it unaware that I was doing it. He disguised all his actions by making them appear as a simple test on a mouse or a program recorded on digital files. You translated his notes. Voss, while you were translating, your mind was being manipulated."

"Come on, Amos, that's absurd. I never translated any information that said Author should be president. He usually gave me a stack of notes and asked me to copy them onto a computer program and then file them into the database we were building."

"And did you read the notes carefully, or did you just copy as instructed?"

"I copied. It wasn't anything I was interested in reading or absorbing; it was mostly scientific jargon, that's all."

"Did you ever wonder why it made no sense to you?"

"No, I concluded it was beyond my paygrade. What would a bunch of $x + y - z$ *chromosome* $w - 2z$ have to do with me? It was just scientific information."

"No, Voss, it was genetic assignments being transferred to your mind. Mind control, Voss, mind control."

"I can't see that, Amos. I never logged in anything that said Author should be president."

"No, you didn't, but what you did log in were certain code assignments that triggered an immediate reaction in your brain when certain terms came up. For instance, when you heard the term 'presidential race' or the word 'president,' your mind immediately jumped to an association that you unconsciously memorized while recording Author's notes. As a result, you said the necessary words, and I quote, 'We should enter Author into the race,' then we all laughed." He pointed his finger at me. "You remember how it happened. We all got quiet at the same time and we assumed that we were all thinking, why not?" He jumped up as if he had suddenly smelled smoke. "We were not having a unified moment of insight. No, our programmed minds all reacted to the assignment, *Enter Author into the race.*" He stomped his foot on the floor as if he had suddenly had a revelation. "That was it, that was the moment, Voss. That was the moment when our programmed assignments kicked in and none of us had any idea that it was happening."

I stared at him, believing and not believing, but part of me knew it was true. "Come on, Amos, are you saying Author was planning to become our president way back then? I can't see anyone planning that far ahead and that meticulously."

He stared at me. "It scares the piss out-a-you, yes?" He got another beer, changed his mind, and took out a platter of cold cuts, neatly arranged and covered with cellophane. "Pat left this for me. She knows I tend to go into a depression sometimes and not eat." He peeled back the clear wrapping and offered me some. "Remember when you were on TV on that Larry Duvall show and you kept going on and on about why Author would make a great president?"

"Yes, I was high on my power to persuade."

"No, Voss, you were fulfilling your programmed assignment."

"You really believe that?"

"I don't just believe it; I know it." He got up and beckoned me to follow him. We went into his office. I expected to see a room full of computers and wires; instead, all I saw was a laptop on a table and a filing cabinet with one drawer hanging open. He sat down at the table and punched in something on the laptop, then he told me to sit down. I did and stared at a computer game. My first thought was that he spent his time playing computer games pretending to be at work.

He logged into the game and told me to play. I stared at him and then started playing the game. It was a simple one of warriors and weapons. I chose a weapon and assumed a character and played my role. I admit, I got caught up in the game and forgot why I was there and what he was trying to prove to me. After I battled an opponent for about twenty minutes, he told me to get up. I was reluctant since I was losing the battle and I wanted to see if I could conquer my opponent and end the game. He logged out and turned the game off. Then he led me to another room where a PC was actively computing something. He invited me to sit down again. He told me to look at the screen.

"That's your brain. I have successfully captured all your mental activity on this program. Now I will briefly alter your thoughts."

"What?"

"Just watch the screen." I looked at the screen and watched as he typed in a few commands. I felt a slight but brief headache and then I felt fine; in fact, I felt good, like I had just had a strong, stimulating drink.

Then he gave me the same weapon I had used in the video game. It was called a kukri, which I learned when I made my weapon of choice. I was shocked, but I accepted it. "You logged in as Luke, right?"

"Good, Luke, take this kukri and go outside and behead my dog. His name is Maxwell; you remember him, right?" I was shocked, but I did not question him. I went straight to the den towards the patio door looking for Max. I saw him outside, gnawing on a bone. I had every intention of slicing his head off. When I got to the door, it was locked and I was upset that I could not get it open to get at the dog. I started beating on the glass. Amos yelled at me, "Voss, stop! Give me the kukri!" I reluctantly surrendered it and sat down shocked. It took me a while to recover. Amos gave me a cup of coffee as I sat there trembling. "I programmed your mind. Voss, you really thought you were Luke the dark warrior, right?"

I nodded my head, ashamed to admit that it was that easy to gain control of my mind.

"What happened to us was not as simple as this demonstration, but it's close. We have been programmed to play his game."

"Do we have a choice? I mean, can we get out?"

"That's what Pat and I have been working on. We were both shocked when we understood what was happening to us. These are recent revelations. Remember, I stopped you by calling out your last name.

That was not your program name; it was a key to get your attention and unhinge you from the program."

I asked for another cup of coffee. "Is it just us, Amos, or are there more programmed people?"

"That's my assignment, Luke. I am supposed to design the program. He sent me his master files and that's how I figured out what was happening to us and how he used us. He asked me to duplicate his program for mass use." He gave me a fresh cup of coffee. "You have my permission to run naked to the lake and drown yourself."

I stared at him. "Is that a command?"

He laughed. "I broke the command; I no longer have any control over you, honest."

"Are you saying that once we know his code language, we can break the control he may have over us?"

"That is my hope." He smiled and slapped me on the back. "Don't take it so hard, Luke; you'll get over it."

Chapter Thirteen

WE SAT AND TALKED FOR A LONG WHILE. I was so exhausted and upset with myself that I asked Amos if I could crash on his sofa. He offered me the guest room; I took a shower and slept until morning. The next day, we went fishing. I thought that was a dumb idea, given all that we were up against, but Amos insisted. It was refreshing to be out on the lake, surrounded by water and fresh air. We caught a few fish and then talked for a long while about how to proceed under existing circumstances.

"Amos, how do you get away with so much anti-Author activity in your home without getting detected? When I'm at home, I walk around tiptoeing like a kid, avoiding the boogie man." Amos laughed as he pulled in his rod. "After your last visit, Pat and I developed a bounce-back blocker. It's a program that acts like a fishing net; it pulls in any and every unwanted signal and bounces them back to the target satellite. We allow some of Author's programs through but not without filtering them so that all he can pick up is what we want him to pick up."

"Man, you could make a fortune with a program like that; why don't you market it and get rich fast?"

"I don't want to get rich fast; I want peace." He opened the cooler and asked me what I wanted. I settled for a bottle of orange juice. "I've been reflecting on all we discussed. I have a possible proposal if you're willing to go through with it."

"I'm open to any and every solution."

"You remember how I said Author has been planning this thing for as far back as any of us can imagine, possibly ever since he was a kid in short pants, yes?"

"That's what you said, and I almost believe you, but I'm not sure if it goes back that far," I replied.

"Nevertheless, we know he's been at this a long time. This allows him a great deal of advantage over all of us and over the whole political world. Our problem is our plans are too short ranged. We react to any visible attack against us, then we settle down and congratulate ourselves, have a party, and celebrate our victory while our enemy plans his next attack."

"That's about the size of it. But we don't know what his next move will be," I argued.

"We do know what it will be. We know he wants world domination. He wants his mind to live forever and become a god: god of politics and god of the whole world. He wants to be worshiped and obeyed at all costs."

"What's that got to do with his next move?"

"You said he wants to borrow your body for a trip to China, right?"

"Yes, that was his request."

"And after that?"

"I suppose he'll think of other reasons to enter my being, probably staying longer and longer until I don't exist and he does."

"He becomes you, and you being healthy with, give or take, sixty or more years of life left. So, he inhabits you for as long as you are useful, then he finds someone else to inhabit, per se. And the cycle goes on, Ad infinitum, yes?"

"That's a long time, but I think that's what he wants, and while living forever, he continues to improve his circuits so that eventually he won't need a body, maybe just a forever brain," I laughed.

Amos opened a cold beer and raised it up to the sun. "Then we destroy the brain."

"You mean to pull the plug on that thing floating in liquid nitrogen? I don't think that will end his reign."

"Probably not, but it might short-circuit his ambitions."

"I don't know, Amos; he's gotten much larger than that wet brain."

"I realize that, but canceling the brain may confuse his plans long enough for us to make our next move."

"Which is?"

He held his beer up to the light. "That answer is in my last sip; I'll know after I swallow it."

Chapter Fourteen

AFTER MY VISIT WITH AMOS, I reflected on the possible steps we discussed. I was running out of time; the president's trip to China was set for the next week and I had not given him a yes or no answer. I kept reviewing what Javier told me about being possessed. I imagined his revolting slimy being entering my person, the thought appalling to me. I resolved in my mind that I would have to tell him no and insist he find another flunkey. I prepared my resignation letter in case it came to either resign or be fired for insubordination. I folded it neatly and placed it in an envelope ready to throw it in his face or light, whichever one was in front of me.

Before my meeting with him, I wanted to inspect some details about what Amos and I had talked about. I wanted to have another look at his confounded brain. I wanted to see if it was possible to disconnect it. Perhaps it was easier than I imagined. Most people thought the Author Project base was at the White House, but I knew that was an illusion created to protect the project and misdirect any would-be attempts at shutting Author down. I went to the old headquarters where Author's brain was floating in liquid nitrogen.

As Author's representative, I had a code to enter every secret place that I knew of. I went into the sacred room where the Author Project was conceived, mapped out, and delivered into sentient life. Amos told me that Author's body was in a temperature control drawer somewhere in that same room, but I did not want to see the body; I assumed he was preserving it for the day his boundless mind figured out how to raise the dead. What I wanted was the great brain, and there it was, looking like a rubber version of a real brain. I studied it carefully, wondering if I should drain off the liquid nitrogen or just unplug the attachments that monitored the brain like a patient on life support. It appeared to be alive with all those wires attached to it, jumpstarting it every few seconds. I rubbed my finger along the edge of the glass case and made a decision. I felt as if someone were watching me, but there was no one in the room. I touched the connecting tubes and wires and wondered which one I should disconnect first. I had not come here to take any definitive action, but it was an opportune time to act; if I resigned from my position as press secretary, I would never get another chance. I stared at the thing for a long while wondering what it would feel like if I touched it. I edged my hand along the flash drive that appeared to feed information into the tank. It would be very easy to jerk it out. I curled my thumb and index finger around the drive, then I was startled by a voice that appeared out of nowhere.

"I wouldn't do that if I were you." I looked around. The voice did not come from the brain but from somewhere in the room or near the container. I moved my hand away; I could feel someone standing directly behind me, breathing slowly. I could smell his favorite tobacco; he was here, if not in the flesh, in the spirit.

"Should I shoot him?" a female voice said.

It was Tenisha; I could recognize that voice anywhere. "Hello, Tenisha. Did you follow me here?" I turned and stared at her. She was dressed in a sexy black suit and a pink low-cut blouse under the jacket. "I see you're dressed for the lab." She smiled and lowered the gun. I did not try to grab it because I knew he was in the room somewhere and I had no idea what kind of physical powers he possessed.

"We've been following you," she said, as she placed the gun on top of the case containing the brain; it would have been so easy to grab it and shoot the container, drain all the liquid out, and let the brain die. Then I remembered, the container was made of clear bulletproof glass. I edged closer to the wires, hoping my left hand could reach the right one and yank it out.

Tenisha stood there smiling at me as if she were waiting for me to kiss her or fall into her arms. Then she pulled off her jacket and slowly began opening her blouse, pearl button by pearl button. I could not believe what I was seeing. What was she up to? I began to weaken and I could feel the force of her sexual powers over me. I was getting hard just watching her actions and my foolish body wanted nothing but what she was offering. I could tell she did not have on a bra or anything under the blouse, which may not matter to some people, but it was damnation to me. I had to fight all my wits to back away from her. She stood there smiling with her blouse open and then she reached her hands behind her back and slowly unzipped her skirt. I imagined the slow process of the zipper sliding down and then she paused before lowering the skirt. "Men are so weak," she said, as she slid out of the skirt wearing nothing but the open blouse and a tiny black thong. I had no idea what to do. I had two guns: one drawn for action and the other waiting on top of the brain case. I chose the other. I grabbed it and pointed it at her half-naked body, and for a moment, she seemed caught off guard. I'd like to think I was strong enough to shoot her, but Author intervened. He somehow materialized behind me and carefully placed his hand over mine. I could feel the firm grip of an athletic young man. He easily peeled my fingers from the trigger and the handle of the gun.

"Now, Luke Adam Voss, why would you want to destroy a beautiful work of art? Look at her, she's Venus on the lab floor. If there is a god, I must give him or her credit for creating a masterpiece. Of course, being part force and part technology, I must say god is probably much like me, or maybe I should rephrase that, maybe god is me and I am god." He laughed as he pressed the muzzle of the gun to the back of my head. "My darling, what is your pleasure? Do you want his head on a platter, or do you want his penis between your legs?" Then he laughed like someone slightly deranged. He pushed me towards her and said, "Sex or death? Your choice."

I stood there like someone about to fall off a cliff and trying to hold onto air. Tenisha smiled and walked slowly towards me, pulling off her blouse in the process. I heard Author sit in the chair near the brain box; I knew he was still holding the gun. I backed sideways away from the box. Author was not looking at me; he had his eyes on Tenisha. Tenisha was nude except for the tiny thong; she was standing there enjoying Author's stare. It was sick. Author had his legs crossed, the gun in one hand, and with the other hand, he was rubbing the brain box. He was so engrossed in the Venus that I made a quick decision to run for the door. I ducked behind the box. If he wanted to shoot me, he would have to risk hitting the brain box. I lowered my body and measured the distance from where I was in relation to the door. There were several obstacles in my path, but that was good; I could use them as shields. I expected him to get up and try to root me out with the gun, but instead, he went over to her and took her in his arms, kissing her passionately. I took that as my opportunity and crawled towards the door. When I thought I was safe, I pushed at the door, hoping it wasn't locked. Instead, I touched something else: his leg. For a hologram, he was very solid. He kicked me on the knee and it hurt badly.

"I gave you a choice, Voss: sex or death. Most men would have no trouble making that decision. What's your problem? Are you the other way inclined?" He grabbed a lab stool and sat down. I could see he was already beginning to fade; his embrace with Tenisha must have knocked his pixels out of whack. He breathed hard for a moment and I was about to strike him when I felt something metal resting on my head. It was Tenisha and she had some kind of metal rod in her hands.

"Touch him and I'll beat your brains out." I looked up at her. She had managed to cover her nakedness with a white lab coat, not sexy but still inviting. I sat there feeling defeated and dizzy from the sexual high I got from just smelling her perfume. Author gave the pistol to her and she sat on the floor, her long legs poised in a lotus position, revealing all I wanted to see. She kept the gun pointed at me while Author mixed some kind of chemical concoction and drank it down. He resumed his position on the stool. Tenisha gave the gun back to him.

"I forget how ignorant you are, Voss, but I'll excuse that in favor of your other qualities." He shook himself like a dog shaking water off his body, his pixels seeming to float in the air and then settle back into his person so that he was as solid as any man and youthful as his college days' self. He smiled at me like a father who was about to explain to his son why he deserves a whipping. "You see, Voss, Tenisha and I want, or shall I say, need a child. Tenisha, of course, is a willing participant, but you, I guess I really don't understand you. I gave up trying ages ago. Perhaps your inability to take advantage of power will one day make rational sense to me. But for now, we have important business to attend to. This is for the good of the country. Tenisha understands that, but you, you are a sad case." He pointed the gun at me again; I was still sitting on the floor hugging my hurt knee. "Sex or death, that was the offer and the offer still stands."

"If you want a child, why don't you go to the sperm bank? I'm sure you can find a worthy candidate with an IQ that matches yours, or you should have taken care of that little detail before you fried your body. What's wrong, you had every other detail planned out, why not that one?"

He laughed, long and hard, and said, "If it was that simple, Voss, we would have gone to the sperm bank long ago. Moreover, I did consider that other detail; unfortunately, in one of my attempts at transferring technology to the human body, I accidentally rendered myself impotent. However, it all worked out for good; I still had plan B: you, Voss. You see, we need more than just a mother and child; we need the third element in a complete family, and what might that be, Mr. Press Secretary?"

I stared at him, feeling helpless, as if I had fallen into a pit that had no bottom and I would be falling forever. "A father," I replied weakly.

He started clapping like a happy teacher, "Bravo, bravo. He understands the ways of the world."

"Why me? I'm sure you could find a thousand men willing to father your child."

He bent over towards me as if he were explaining arithmetic to a dog. "I selected you years ago. Just like God selected Abraham to be the patriarch of his people, I selected you to be the father of my future son." He nudged the gun to my ear. "And you thought I just liked you and wanted to give you a job. No, fate assisted me in selecting you. You had the misfortune of being paired with me in college, and I had the fortune of seeing your genetic worth and your perfect match for my plan. Do you think I suddenly had an epiphany and decided to do all this one happy day? No, my friend, this has been a long-range plan. I have been dreaming this up all my life. Since I was a child, I was carefully selecting and planning my every move to get to the place where I am now. For every person I allowed in my life, I screened and carefully matched them to my plans. You," he pointed the gun at me. "Tenisha, my lovely darling, Amos, Kim, Pat, Javier, all of you were carefully selected to help implement my long-range goals." He kicked at my leg, "Don't you understand you can't fight against God?"

"You're not God."

He burst out laughing, "Darling, tell him who I am."

She smiled at him beaming, "You're God."

"Haven't you wondered what the C stands for in my middle name? I bet you thought it was for Charles," he made a clicking sound with his tongue. "Luke, you should be careful how you approach your god. Please don't encourage my wrath."

He placed the gun in his belt and clapped his hands together. "OK, let's get down to business. No better place to conceive a future president than right here," he tapped the brain box, "in the presence of the great mind." He stood up, smiled at Tenisha, and said, "Are you ready, my dear? I'm sure Luke has the good sense to choose life."

Chapter Fifteen

THAT WAS A FEW YEARS AGO. Tenisha's eager eggs were delighted to receive my sperm. I won't go into the details of that sordid sexual encounter, as sex at gunpoint is no fun. I agreed to marry her with the stipulation that he never again witness our lovemaking. He accepted the terms. It has been much better since then. In choosing life, I had to accept all that goes with life. I am a proud father of a happy, healthy, highly intelligent boy. We, of course, named him in honor of Author, as many other mothers have named their sons.

You might say I sold out, but I don't see it that way. I placed myself in an auspicious position to observe him and keep an eye on his activities, which are more sinister than I realized. Obviously, much of the country loves him; after all, he resolved the national debt. We no longer owe China; China owes us. As I mentioned in my press conference, he sold our national secrets to China and any other willing country that wanted a piece of the action. He sold our latest drone technology; he sold our fighter jet's technology and a host of other things for top dollars. Moreover, he convinced Americans that all those pennies children sent in added up to help resolve the national debt. Little children are running around thinking they alone resolved the national debt. They are having penny drives to keep the nation debt free forever. That's one of his mottos, *Debt Free Forever.*

I see him often. He comes over like a proud grandfather to see his grandson. I asked him how he justified selling the country to China. He laughed and said our technology was outdated and everything is being replaced with new cutting-edge designs, far more sophisticated than the old models. He said he has already sent advanced weapons technology models to the Pentagon for production and implementation at various manufacturing plants across the country. He claims we are so far ahead of the game, we will soon own the world. Actually, he already does; he has planted little Authors in most major Western countries, waiting to be set in motion at the right time. He has only two years left in his second term, and at his request, I am planning my campaign for president when he steps down. He has already hinted that he will be endorsing me as his replacement.

Don't get me wrong, I still plan to destroy him as soon as I get enough evidence to expose him. I am planning to wait until I win the presidency. I confess there are times when I feel as if I am thinking like Author, but when that happens, I remind myself that I am Luke Adam Voss, and I remember my dossier that I plan to release right after I take the oath of office. Author does not know about this and I don't plan to tell him. Possession is a gradual thing; it never happens overnight; sometimes it takes years, and as long as I keep a clear mind, I can still be me.

Author is tenacious in his planning. Tenisha is now working on her PhD in political science and I am committed to studying political affairs throughout the world. We are a typical postmodern American family, devoted to the Author Project, sometimes called, Author Family Planning. He wants America to remain on top of the world in every field. Everyone who signs up for the Author Family Plan is encouraged to send their children to the best schools with a promise of free university tuition if they remain in the plan. Author encourages large families and equal opportunity for all children to ensure an endless supply of bright minds to run the country and develop advanced technology in all fields as well as futuristic plans for those interested in new artistic forms.

Sometimes I am deceived into thinking Author is a benevolent mastermind, but overall, I see him as an evil tyrant slowly taking over the world. You might ask why I question his wisdom, given all the advances we have seen in our country and in social and political relations since he took office. However, history attests that most dictators start out as noble leaders who eventually turn on the people they claim to love. And I am convinced Author loves no one except himself and his power base. As much as he dotes over Tenisha and our children, I know it is not love but one more form of absolute control. I'm sure if he was still a man, he would possibly be infatuated with Tenisha and he would probably find her sexually desirable. But I know for a fact he is using her to birth his progeny. Even though our children are our progenies, he claimed them as soon as they were born, as if we were only surrogate parents he paid to have his babies. Tenisha is still infatuated with him, but I sense she is beginning to see through his ostensible electric love. I have witnessed them kissing behind a bush or teasing each other in the pantry, but there is no flesh in his lovemaking, literally and physically. I've witnessed how he looks at Tenisha when she's not aware of his stare, almost like a kind of loathing. Perhaps at first, he really was infatuated with her, but I am convinced the woman he needs does not exist in this world. Perhaps he is inventing her in his warped mind, and one day, he will use Tenisha as a model for what he really wants but with more desirable apps that will turn him on in his mechanical construct.

I mentioned this to Tenisha and she stopped speaking to me for a week. But I know I hit a nerve and she resented me for doing that. I was so sick of him hanging out at my home in his multi-pixelated form that I cursed him out one day and he disappeared for a good while until the children started asking when Grandpa Author would be back. I believe Tenisha is falling in love with me, or maybe Author has convinced her to spend more time with me. I can't say, but she has been cozying up to me a lot lately. Probably she wants to know what I do on my weekends away from her and the kids. Possibly she thinks I have an outside woman, but I dispel that notion whenever I make love to her. I don't trust her; I believe Author has her spying on me. He wants to know what I am keeping from him, but he is reluctant to ask me since he knows I will only laugh in his pixeled face. I also think my newfound confidence troubles him a great deal. It was easier for him to manipulate me when I was trembling at the monster we had created. But now I find him amusing. My confidence surprised me, but I think it came from thinking of my mother and how much she believed in me. When I told her I was not interested in being a doctor, she was disappointed, but she told me to be the best at whatever I decided to do with my life. "That's all I ask of you," I remember her saying.

It was a pleasure to see Author staring at me with that questioning look on his face. Author may have a great deal of knowledge, more knowledge than I can fathom, but he lacks one important ingredient: he has no real feelings. I don't think he had real feelings even when he was alive. What he had was an excessive amount of determination and willpower. When he stared at me the way he did, I realized he resented my emotions and feelings. He tried, but he could never get to that level of love and caring. And that is the major difference between us.

I recognize that there is an extremely dark side to Author, an evil I cannot begin to describe or discuss on these pages. For instance, consider all those bright little children he is sending off to pre-university training facilities compliments of the Author Family Plan. I fear those children are being brainwashed into not only studying advanced genetic technology, but I believe they are also being used as lab rats to test his theories and expand his knowledge of genetics and the human mind. Believe me, computer babies are not just children who are fascinated with, and obsessed with, studying genetics; they are also allowing themselves to be experimented on to advance the cause of science and technology, all at the encouragement of the great Author and their deceived families.

He now has a special children's channel called TGM, Technology for Growing Minds. These are not, Let's Learn Our ABCs and Let's Count to Ten programs; the cartoons and computer-generated images contain information parents and the average adult cannot understand. Author insists that learning technology and genetics is as simple for children as learning a foreign language.

I keep up with the data his cyber mind spits out; it is often computer-generated comparative analyses of children's reactions to various tests and cognitive analysis programs. Tenisha and I have argued about how much advanced technological learning we should allow our children, and as always, she sides with Author, as if they are his children instead of mine. She and Author insist that our family must be the model for the country; they claim that people are looking to us to set the standard for early advanced education for the children of America.

Tenisha agrees with everything Author says. Just when I think she's coming to her senses and realizes he is a fraud, he shows up, dazzling her with gifts and showers of attention that she misinterprets as love. I get truly angry when she gives him that look that implies she wants him more than she wants me. He has improved his cocktail mixture of chemicals that allows him to appear more and more like the youthful college boy. Furthermore, his pixels seem to be lasting longer, so he hangs around my family more than I care to see him. In support of the Author Family Planning Guide, Tenisha is pregnant with our third child. I confess I am worried about the future of our children. I don't trust Author; he spends far too much time with our son, teaching him things I feel he is too young to understand or make quality responsible decisions about. Our daughter is too young to understand that Grandpa Author is not a real person. She enjoys the multicolored lights that he dazzles her with, but that will change when she begins to realize what Author really is. Tenisha insists I not tell her or our son about the real nature of Grandpa Author. She said she was leaving that for Author to do. Irrational woman, I wonder what lies she expects Author to spin for them.

Even more frightening to me is the fact that some of the opposition groups have accepted Author as a wise leader and even consider him a friend of the people. The media no longer pursues me for proof that Author is a dictator, but instead, they want the latest on Author's next great idea to modernize and improve the country. Personally, I fear I have lost my case before I have had the opportunity to expose him. Nevertheless, that does not prevent me from keeping this memoir with plans to release it when necessary.

To prevent sabotage, I deposit monthly copies of my writing in a safe deposit box in an unnamed city and I mail copies to an underground group assisting me in my Author Watch Program. They know what to do when it is necessary to act. After all, not everyone in the country is deceived and we believe there is a way to defeat Author. I plan to do that even if it means destroying myself for the sake of the country. My former Author Project teammates are secretly on my side, minus Tenisha. We hold secret meetings whenever we can and we have a growing underground network of supporters. When I take over as president, we plan to expose Author C. Owen. In the meantime, I am going along with his proposals. What else can I do? He practically lives in my house and often follows me around, as if he does not trust me to be alone with Tenisha and our children. But at least I can keep a watchful eye on him. I could use a dry martini right now.

Acknowledgments

Thank you to my friends and fellow writers who support my writing and encourage all my efforts. A special thanks to the poetry communities in New Orleans and Baton Rouge and the Augusta Poetry group in Augusta, GA.

Thank you to My Sister Prayer Group where we nourish impossible dreams.

Author Bio

Malaika Favorite is a visual artist and writer. Her publications include: *Dreaming at the Manor* (Finishing Line Press, 2014) and *Illuminated Manuscript* (New Orleans Poetry Journal Press, 1991). Malaika won the 2015 Broadside Lotus Press Naomi Long Madgett Poetry Award for her collection of poems, *Ascension*. Her poetry, fiction, and articles have appeared in numerous anthologies and journals. An interview with Malaika was featured in the Fall 2014 issue of *Xavier Review*, and her article on art was included in an issue of *The Southern Quarterly*. As a visual artist, Malaika received her BFA (1971) and MFA (1973) in art from LSU Baton Rouge, LA. Her artwork is featured in: *Art: African American* by Samella Lewis, *African American Art and Artist*, also by Samella Lewis, *Black Art in Louisiana* by Bernardine B. Proctor, and the *St. James Guide to Black Artists*, by Thomas Riggs. Her works are in the following collections: Absolut Vodka, Morris Museum of Art, Augusta, GA; Alexandria Museum of Art, Alexandria, LA.; The Coca Cola Company, Atlanta, GA.; Hartsfield Jackson International Airport, Atlanta, GA, and The National Underground Railroad Freedom Center, Cincinnati, Ohio. She has two commissioned outdoor murals in Atlanta, GA, one on Auburn Ave. (2007) and another on White Street (2009).